Thanks

A BOTANIC HILL DETECT

MW00791494

EUCALYPTUS STREET:

GREEN CURSE

Seek out what is hidden with courage and BY _wisdom._

SHERRILL JOSEPH

♡ _Sherrill Joseph_

10/23/2020

ACORN PUBLISHING

FROM THE TINY ACORN...
GROWS THE MIGHTY OAK

Eucalyptus Street: Green Curse. First Edition

Copyright © 2020 Sherrill M. Joseph. All rights reserved.

Printed in the United States of America. For information, address Acorn Publishing, LLC, 3943 Irvine Blvd. Ste. 218, Irvine, CA 92602

www.acornpublishingllc.com

Cover design by eBook Launch

Digital Formatting and Interior Design by Debra Cranfield Kennedy

Family Tree by Ellen Goodwin, Ellen Goodwin Graphics

Library of Congress Control Number: 2020916920

ISBN: 978-1-952112-13-3

Dedicated to my granddaughter, Chloe,

One of the sweetest, most curious kids I've ever known.

Books can be magic carpets to enchanted lands.

Happy lifelong reading, Cupcake.

Love always from your Gigi XOXO

Full many a gem of purest ray serene,

The dark unfathomed caves of ocean bear:

Full many a flower is born to blush unseen,

And waste its sweetness on the desert air.

Thomas Gray, English poet
From "Elegy Written in a Country
Churchyard," published in 1751

CONTENTS

EUCALYPTUS STREET:

GREEN CURSE

Other Botanic Hill Detectives Mysteries:

Book 1 – NUTMEG STREET: Egyptian Secrets

THE DE CORDOBA FAMILY TREE

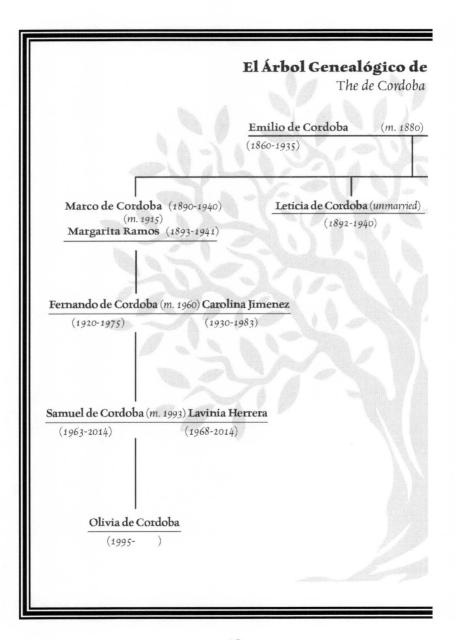

El Árbol Genealógico de
The de Cordoba

Emilio de Cordoba   *(m. 1880)*
(1860-1935)

Marco de Cordoba (1890-1940)   Leticia de Cordoba *(unmarried)*
        (m. 1915)   (1892-1940)
Margarita Ramos (1893-1941)

Fernando de Cordoba *(m. 1960)* Carolina Jimenez
(1920-1975)   (1930-1983)

Samuel de Cordoba *(m. 1993)* Lavinia Herrera
(1963-2014)   (1968-2014)

Olivia de Cordoba
(1995-   )

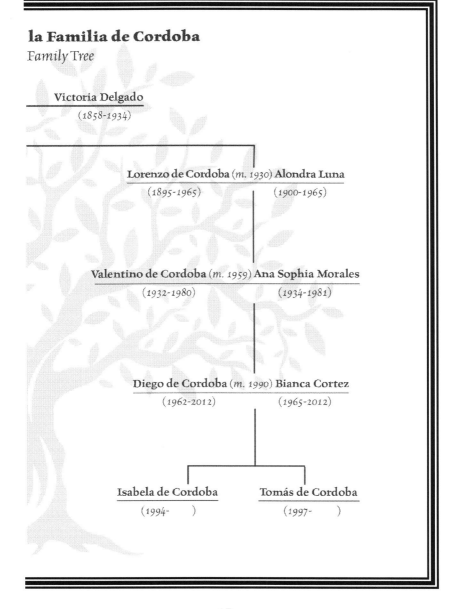

la Familia de Cordoba
Family Tree

Victoria Delgado
(1858-1934)

Lorenzo de Cordoba (*m. 1930*) Alondra Luna
(1895-1965)   (1900-1965)

Valentino de Cordoba (*m. 1959*) Ana Sophia Morales
(1932-1980)   (1934-1981)

Diego de Cordoba (*m. 1990*) Bianca Cortez
(1962-2012)   (1965-2012)

Isabela de Cordoba   Tomás de Cordoba
(1994-   )   (1997-   )

CHAPTER ONE

· ✧ ·

A Mystery from Eucalyptus Street

A tremendous thunderclap propelled thirteen-year-old Lanny Wyatt right off the plush living room sofa. He had been dozing there after a heavy dinner, mesmerized by the drumming rain outside and the fire roaring in the enormous fireplace of the historic mansion on Eucalyptus Street. The immense estate had once belonged to an old-time Hollywood actor and actress. Their portraits, among others, had been staring down at him. Earlier he'd thought it was funny that the portraits' eyes seemed to follow him around the room . . . but later, lying on his backside, not so much. The thunderclap was the final straw. He had scrambled to his feet.

Lanny walked toward the floor-to-ceiling French doors and squinted through their tiny square glass panes. Beyond the flagstone patio, on the estate grounds, he noticed darkness had overtaken the old, windswept eucalyptus trees.

Sheets of rain were blowing sideways, pelting and rattling the mansion's windows. For split seconds, lightning illuminated the foliage with eerie strobe-like effects, giving the trees and expansive, rolling lawns a surreal, colorless appearance. This was the kind of night anything could happen.

Lanny knew raging storms such as this were unusual in his coastal, Southern California hometown of Las Palmitas, especially in September. It was the perfect way to begin a new mystery.

As if reading Lanny's mind, his twin sister, Lexi, joined him in checking out the downpour. Their friends Moki Kalani and Rani Kumar, also thirteen, followed her into the room. Almost in a whisper, Lexi said, "Some cool storm, huh? And we finally got inside this famous old house. Plus, we have a new mystery, all in one night." Lexi beamed ear-to-ear as she pushed aside the sheer curtain for a better view.

"This storm is nothing compared with those in Hawai'i," said Moki. "Palm trees come crashing down everywhere." He and his widowed father had moved to California from O'ahu when the now tall, muscular boy was a scrawny eight-year-old. Moki slapped his best friend Lanny on the back. "Not as exciting as a Honolulu hurricane, bro, but still fun."

"If this was India, there'd be venomous snakes slithering in through cracks under the doors," said Rani. The slim girl and her parents came to live in Las Palmitas from India when she was five. Rani and Lexi had become best friends instantly.

At that moment, a flash of lightning made Rani's peach-color sequined sari sparkle. She liked wearing saris to honor her culture as well as her grandmother who made them for her. Rani also enjoyed playfully taunting Moki, and her snake story did a nice job of it.

"Ooh, no more snakes, please," he said. "I had enough of them in our first mystery to give me nightmares for a lifetime."

Moki wasn't exaggerating. He and his three friends, who called themselves the Botanic Hill Detectives, had just dodged venomous snakes and brazen, masked characters to successfully conclude their first dangerous case, *Nutmeg Street: Egyptian Secrets*. Using brains, technology, and patience, the mature teens discovered who really stole an ancient Egyptian burial urn. The squad found the urn, brought the real thieves to justice, and restored the formerly spotless reputation of their friend, world-famous Egyptologist Dr. Winston Thornsley. His untimely death had been caused by being falsely accused of the artifact's theft. All those matters were set right now, so they were about to hear their new case.

The echo of high heels clicking on the mansion's tiled entryway caused the four kids to turn their attention toward their hostess, the home's current owner, Isabela de Cordoba. Two of the portraits with the creepy eyeballs were of her great-great-grandparents, Emilio de Cordoba and Victoria Delgado. They had built the family mansion, *La Casa de los Árboles*, or "The House of the Trees," in 1885. Isabela had inherited the property and turned it into a museum of sorts to honor her distinguished family. The fashionable, young woman had just come downstairs to rejoin her guests.

"Sorry for the delay, kids. I found the items I wanted to read to you. Strange, but the envelope wasn't where I thought I had left it this afternoon. Anyway, I'm so pleased you detectives are my neighbors. And grateful you've accepted my invitation to stay here as my guests. We must find my family's long-lost emerald. And the noises—I need to know who or what's responsible for the unexplained noises and happenings inside my home and around the grounds."

"Well, I have to be honest with you, Ms. de Cordoba," Moki started. The woman seemed young enough for the kids to call "Isabela," but they didn't dare. Their parents had raised them to be polite to adults, and even if she seemed barely old enough to be out of college, she owned a mansion, so she was plenty "adult" to them. So it was Ms. de Cordoba, all the way.

"The thing is," Moki continued, "we wouldn't have missed this chance for anything. The only time we've ever been able to see inside this huge house was from your doorway while trick-or-treating. By the way, thanks for always passing out the best Halloween candy on Botanic Hill."

Lexi elbowed Moki in the ribs and added quickly, "And we've always been curious about this house and your family, what with our love of mysteries."

"Why, thank you so much, Alexia," Isabela replied.

"Uh, would you please just call me by my nickname 'Lexi'?"

"Of course, Lexi. But how about your brother? It's Lanyon, no?"

"Lanny, please," he said, hoping to avoid being endlessly teased by Moki over his real name. "I like old houses, but your home's connection to classic Hollywood movies makes it especially interesting." If he could go back in time, Lanny knew he would be a silent film star of the 1920s and '30s, playing classic detective parts. He had a collection of those black-and-white films and watched them over and over. "Now *that*'s detecting," he'd always say.

"Be warned, Ms. de Cordoba," Rani said. "Lanny's quite the authority on old Hollywood."

Isabela clasped her hands. "Fabulous. His knowledge might come in handy, so I'd call this a win-win situation. But now, let's settle in, and I'll tell you the story of this old estate and its mysteries."

CHAPTER TWO

· ✧ ·

Emeralds and Ancestors

Isabela directed the four kids back toward the opulent but comfortable sofa and chairs. The fireplace and the lightning still crackled in concert with the driving rain and wuthering winds. Everyone took a seat, anxious to hear the details of their new case.

"My great-great grandparents were originally from Spain and settled in Mexico where they did very well in the silver and gemstone mining business. That enabled them to come here to California and purchase this large piece of property we now enjoy. Back then, this section of Las Palmitas was almost completely covered with eucalyptus tree groves."

"Oh, yeah," Lexi said. "Eucalyptus trees were brought here from Australia. People building railroads during the California Gold Rush thought the trees would make good railroad track ties."

Lanny said, "But the young wood cracked and decayed

as it dried." He shook his head, then raked back the dark blond curls that had fallen onto his forehead.

Rani snapped her fingers. "So that's how this street on Botanic Hill got named Eucalyptus Street."

"Yes," Isabela said. "I love eucalyptus trees though they can be quite dangerous, especially in storms like the one this evening. They're known to have shallow roots, which means they can easily and dangerously topple.

"Anyway, my great-great-grandparents raised their three children here at the *casa*. The youngest was my great-grandfather, the Hollywood actor Lorenzo de Cordoba.

"This *casa*—I mean 'house'—became Lorenzo's when his parents died since his brother and sister had left the country to mine emeralds in India and never returned. When Lorenzo passed away, the house went to his son, my grandfather. But my family always lived together in this spacious home as a happy extended family. Even my cousin Olivia lived here. But when her parents died last year in a plane crash, she decided she wanted no part of it—or the family—anymore. She grew convinced that the estate and the whole family were cursed. She took off, and the last I heard, she'd moved to Europe for college."

"Cursed? That's fascinating," Rani said. She leaned forward like Lexi, who was as quietly as possible inhaling Isabela's expensive, spicy perfume.

"We'll definitely get to 'The Curse' in a few minutes."

"Your only cousin has left, so the house is all yours?" Moki asked.

"Well, mine and my younger brother, Tomás's. You'll meet him soon."

"Cool," Moki said. He peered around, wondering what it would be like to inherit such an amazing house.

"Why didn't Lorenzo go to India with his brother and sister to mine for emeralds?" Rani asked. "India's awesome and famous for those gorgeous green gemstones, you know." She got a faraway look in her eyes as she often did when she missed her old country.

"He was about to marry the silent-movie actress Alondra Luna and was interested in furthering his own acting career up in Hollywood."

"So, the emerald we're supposed to be looking for was found in India?" Lexi nudged. She gave a little shiver when she looked toward the window that was still being blitzed by the rainstorm.

"Yes. According to family stories, sometime in the 1940s, Lorenzo received an ordinary-looking package in the mail from his sister, Leticia, in India. When he opened it, he found to his astonishment that it contained a round, flawless emerald about the size of an apricot, already faceted and polished, even then worth over a million dollars. The note inside the package said that she and her brother, Marco, had found it in Northern India and had named it 'The Leticia Emerald.'

"Leticia's note also said that he was to keep the gem safe and a secret until the two returned to the States. If anything happened to her, she wanted Lorenzo, her favorite brother, to inherit the stone. Well, tragically, neither Leticia nor Marco ever returned to Las Palmitas. Both were reportedly drowned during a boating accident on the Ganges River. Their bodies were never recovered."

Moki gulped. "Wow. What an adventure. So, part of what we're looking for is a humongous, expensive emerald."

"Yes, as well as what's causing the mysterious disturbances here." Isabela pushed some errant, dark strands of hair back into the bun at her neckline, then continued.

"Family legends say my great-grandfather feared his *siblings* had stolen the stone themselves from somewhere in India. Whom they'd taken it from, no one could guess. Supposedly, Lorenzo and his wife didn't know what else to do with an emerald that might have been stolen, so they hid it." She chuckled and glanced up at their portraits. "Being actors, my great-grandparents did have a flair for the dramatic. Anyway, down through the generations, we heard it might be hidden somewhere on this property. But, as to where and why, exactly, no one knew for sure. Many family members over the years have searched the house and grounds for the emerald, but it's never been found."

"But isn't it possible after all these years that the emerald could have been stolen from your estate?" Lanny asked.

"I'm almost certain it's still here—as you will soon understand," she replied. Lanny's blue-violet eyes opened wide. But he'd have to wait. Rani had a question.

"So, where does the curse your cousin Olivia referred to come in?"

"Ah, that's the tragic part, Rani." Isabela bit her lip, then continued. "Nearly every member of my family has died accidentally, suddenly, or at a relatively young age. You probably know that both Lorenzo and his wife, Alondra, died in 1965 when the movie set they were shooting on one day mysteriously burst into flames. They were trapped and killed by falling debris. Then, my grandparents Valentino and Ana Sophia died one year apart in the 1980s after contracting a deadly disease from a trip to Africa. So, sadly, I never knew either of them. My own parents, Diego and Bianca, died a few years ago in a car crash. Cousin Olivia labeled these tragedies 'The Green Curse' because she was convinced the numerous family deaths had to have been caused by the emerald. Amazingly, the series of accidental deaths did start after the family took possession of the gemstone in the 1940s."

Lanny rose to his feet once again. "Talk about a family story. So, how do you know the emerald is probably still somewhere on the estate? What's happened recently to make you want us to find it now? And are you sure you really want to?"

"Great questions, Lanny. That's where this comes in." Isabela waved a thick yellowed envelope in the air. "I received an unexpected call two days ago from an attorney, a Mr. Troy Landis. He's a partner in a long-established law firm here in town. He said he would be giving me a 'secret letter' written to me by my great-grandfather Lorenzo—more correctly, written to 'Lorenzo and Alondra's eldest descendant three generations hence' and to be presented by an attorney on that person's twenty-first birthday. My birthday. Apparently unknown to the rest of my family, the letter's been in the law firm's vault since 1945.

"Mr. Landis personally placed the envelope in my hands yesterday when I turned twenty-one. My brother, Tomás, is only eighteen, and Cousin Olivia won't be twenty-one until next year. Sadly, we are the last of the de Cordobas. So, this secret letter is definitely mine."

The four kids noticed Isabela's momentary melancholy and wished her a happy belated birthday. Then, they sat speechless because of her incredible story and out of respect for her feelings. They also didn't want to delay for another second Isabela's reading of the contents of the birthday envelope. Lanny was especially excited, knowing he was about to hear the words of an actor he greatly admired. The young woman carefully unfolded one document and began.

"This is the letter, dated May 10, 1945." Isabela smoothed the crispy pages and read the following:

"My dearest and eldest descendant of your generation—Heartfelt greetings to you on this, your twenty-first birthday. I hope you are actually reading this at La Casa de los Árboles, our noble family casa. If only I could be there with you and know you. I am certain I would be proud.

You are no doubt wondering why you are receiving a letter today from your long-deceased relative. No doubt you have also heard many stories down through the decades about "The Leticia Emerald" that was found in India. The emerald is indeed the primary focus of this letter.

I received the emerald in the mail from my sister, Leticia, who was in India in 1940. In the last five years, I have been unable to determine whether or not my brother and sister were ever the legal owners of the stone. This has haunted my dear wife, Alondra, and me to the point where we recently decided to hide the emerald for the rest of our lifetime and the lifetimes of the family's next two generations. Hopefully, by the third generation descended from me, of which you are a part, some information will have come to light as to where and to whom the emerald truly belongs.

You are hereby charged with finding it if you choose—a Birthday Treasure Hunt, so to speak. My hope is that the stone will be returned to its rightful owner if our family is not legally entitled to it. But if you find it, you may do with it as you wish—keep it, sell it, or find its rightful owner, etc.

I am revealing to you now that it has been hidden somewhere within our noble family casa or on its grounds. But to assist you further, I have enclosed a puzzle poem I *composed. It contains clues to help you in your search. Decipher the clues, and you should be able to find the treasure.*

You must be asking yourself by now why I am making a game of this instead of telling you outright where the emerald is located. A fair question. Perhaps the actor in me is having some fun. But the real reason is that I partially hope the emerald stays hidden. I can't predict the future, but something tells me nothing good will come from our family having the gemstone in hand.

But I also understand such a valuable stone—100 carats, faceted, and worth over a million dollars today in 1945— might have a monetary value or purpose for you I cannot currently perceive. Again, find it if you can, and it's yours to dispose of or to keep at your discretion.

I hope you will eventually be grateful for this opportunity I have bestowed upon you and not despise your old relative who will eternally have the family's best interest at heart. I wish I could watch the search. Good luck.

Your loving relative, Lorenzo de Cordoba."

"Wow. For a silent movie star, he sure had a way with words," Lexi said with her green eyes fixated on the letter Isabela was slowly lowering to her lap.

"Actually," Lanny said, "Lorenzo de Cordoba and Alondra Luna transitioned well from silent movies in the '20s to 'talkies' in the '30s. You know—*talkies*. Pictures with sound."

Moki rolled his eyes. "Oh, here we go already. 'Lanny the Lexicon' is blasting off." It was true. Lanny was proud to be a walking dictionary as well as an old-movie buff.

His best friend's endless teasing never stopped him.

Rani blinked and sighed, disappointed to return to reality after the fantastic story. "Well, Moki, maybe Lanny's knowledge of Old Hollywood *will* come in very handy on this case. And you know, there's nothing wrong with anyone increasing their word power."

Lanny's eyes grew in size at the same rate as his smile, both directed at Rani.

Lexi, always intrigued by poetry, asked Isabela, "But where's the puzzle poem your great-grandfather mentioned? And could you be more specific about the strange noises and happenings that have been bothering you?"

"Let's start with the puzzle poem." Isabela shuffled the pages to get to it.

She was about to share it with her four guests when she startled them by going silent. Her brown eyes grew large as she slowly glanced upward. The detective squad did the same, not knowing why at first, noticing only the colorful fresco of birds and trees painted on the high ceiling. Tongues of firelight from the tall, cavernous fireplace created an eerie shadow dance that seemed to animate the fantastical figures above.

"Wait . . . listen!" Isabela whispered as she put her trembling finger to her lips. A few seconds later, she asked, "Don't you hear that?" She looked from face to face.

"Hear what?" asked Moki. He shifted his gaze from the ceiling to around the room.

But before anyone else could speak again, heavy footsteps were clearly heard overhead. A little shiver ran through Lexi—but not from the pouring rain this time.

"Who else is in the house?" Lanny asked. "And what room is directly above us?"

"No one else. We five are the only ones home. It's my bedroom up there." Isabela pointed upward and swallowed hard. "This isn't the first time this has happened."

"Then come on," Lexi said. She had regained her courage and bounded out of her chair. "We're going to begin our case by finding out who Big Foot is."

CHAPTER THREE

· ✧ ·

Mysterious Footsteps

L exi led the charge into the entryway and toward the grand staircase that curved up the walls. Rani hiked up her sari and soon overtook her friend. The others bolted up the stairs silently two at a time, not even bothering to hold onto the wrought iron banister. They were on the second floor in a flash to find the source of the eerie footsteps. Isabela followed closely, now clutching her high heels in hand together with the letter and poem. She lifted the shoes, using them to point the kids in the right direction to her bedroom door once they were all in the long hallway.

The two girls were the first to burst into the lavender-scented room. Soft amber light from a small nightstand lamp barely illuminated the area. On first inspection, no intruder was to be seen.

The kids quickly and fearlessly fanned out with Isabela's nodded permission, searching the large walk-in closet, master bathroom, mirrored dressing room, even under the king-sized bed, and behind the heavy brocade window curtains. Whoever or whatever had made the footsteps had vanished, seemingly without a trace.

Rather than move a dressing screen to look behind it, Moki stood on a low upholstered footstool to look over the top. He stayed a few seconds too long. Snap went its leg! He managed to jump to the floor safely, but the stool's limb was broken in half. *What a dope*, he said to himself. His dad was always telling him to be careful around furniture. He could feel his face get hot as he bent and picked up the broken piece to take to Isabela. "Sorry about this, Ms. de Cordoba. I have some great glue at my house to fix it."

"Oh, dear!" Isabela said. One look at her pained face, and Moki knew he had made a bad decision to climb on it. "That footstool was my mother's. Please be careful in this house, Moki. Its contents are precious to me. They're all I have left of my beloved family."

With pursed lips, she snatched the piece from his hand, wrapped it in a tissue, and placed it gently into her nightstand drawer. Moki shuffled his feet, then looked up at Lexi, who gave him a sympathetic glance.

From the commotion, Lanny's attention was drawn to the lamp on the nightstand. Pointing to it, he asked, "Ms. de Cordoba, did you leave that light on?"

"Come to think of it, no, I didn't. That proves the noise wasn't my imagination." Her voice was trembling. "How maddening. There's no way an intruder could've gotten out of here without passing us in the hall. And it's too long a drop out the window. This is so baffling." She made a few steps toward one of the room's many windows.

"Do you have a burglar alarm?" Moki asked. He idly sat down on Isabela's pink satin bedspread, rumpling it, but Lexi yanked him off and smoothed it with both hands before Isabela could notice and comment that it was too expensive to sit on.

She faced the kids. "Yes, and the alarm is on, even when I'm home. We have so many family antiques and objects of personal, sentimental value that must be protected. Since the alarm hasn't been triggered lately, I can't help but suspect someone knows the new passcode— or another way into this house."

"Those are great deductions," Lanny said. He then looked around the room. "Who does know the code?"

"Just my brother and I."

"Could your brother have given it to anyone?" Rani asked.

"No. Tomás is forever cautioning me not to reveal it. And I have taken his advice."

"Um, I have a question . . ." Lexi said. "Ms. de Cordoba, do you believe in 'The Green Curse' yourself as your cousin Olivia seems to?"

"Not at all. I'm not a superstitious person."

"So, you don't think it will make any difference to the lives of you and your two remaining family members if the emerald is found as opposed to it staying hidden?" Lexi asked.

"That's right. It's already been hidden for over

seventy years, and look at all the deaths that have occurred. I doubt bringing it out of hiding could make things worse."

"Speaking of hiding," said Moki, "where's Rani?"

Everyone spun around and scanned the room.

"Rani!" Lexi called out with a catch in her voice. She often worried about her BFF because Rani was small. This made Lexi fear perhaps unrealistically that her friend might be more easily lost, or worse—crushed or trampled in a crowd. With all Rani's ballet classes, swimming and yoga lessons, and natural athleticism, she'd grown so flexible and light on her feet that her friends "lost" her all the time. This added to Lexi's concern.

"Rani's around the corner," Rani called out in a muffled voice a few seconds later. She tended to do this, wander off just beyond everyone's sight, when her curiosity took over. "Come see this," she called more loudly. Her voice came from right past one of the nearer walls and smaller spaces in Isabela's bedroom that seemed to go on forever.

"Thank goodness!" Lexi moved quickly toward the sound.

The others followed Lexi and found Rani within a small alcove, or wall indentation, that was the perfect place for a dainty writing desk. One of its polished mahogany drawers had been left open. Rani pointed and asked, "Did you leave it that way, Ms. de Cordoba?"

"No. I distinctly remember closing that drawer after I opened it when I came up here to look for the envelope from Mr. Landis. That was where I thought I'd put it, but it wasn't there. Remember I mentioned something like that to you?"

Moki nodded. "Yes, when you came back downstairs with the envelope. Where did you actually find it?"

"The envelope was there on the floor under my desk." Isabela pointed to the spot.

"So, this is just a theory," said Lanny, "but it seems logical to me that whoever was in here just now was also here earlier. You probably interrupted the person's search when you came up here a while ago to get the envelope. The intruder had probably just found it but heard you coming and dropped it in order to hide or escape. Then they came out of hiding or returned a few minutes ago to get the envelope, forgetting it wasn't in the desk drawer. The person opened the drawer but noticed it was gone and, before leaving, decided to have a little fun by trying to scare us."

Lexi frowned. "I think Lanny's on to something. If that's true, my big question is, how does the person enter and escape unseen? And where do they go?"

Rani's palms were upturned. "But are we sure the person is really gone? I think the intruder has a secret hiding place, so we should probably search the rest of this floor."

Isabela sighed. "No need. I've searched every time, but there's never anything or anyone to be found. Even the police have searched with no results."

"Wow, Ms. de Cordoba. That was brave of you,"

Moki said. "I don't think I could go poking around in such a huge house all by myself."

"Well, thank you, Moki, but usually, it's more anger than courage. The noises go away just long enough for me to relax. Then, I get scared all over again when I hear them the next time."

"The brave one in my family is my dad, Sergeant Dan Kalani. He's with the Las Palmitas Police Department," Moki said with a big grin. "Would you like me to call him to come over personally and investigate?"

"Thanks, Moki, but not tonight. Though I'd like to meet him. We can call him if we have any further disturbances. I'm actually kind of embarrassed about calling the police again. I bet I already have a reputation within your father's department as 'the girl who cried wolf.'" Isabela attempted a little laugh to ease the tension.

Moki started to ask what "the girl who cried wolf" meant, but Lexi elbowed him to prevent Lanny from giving them a vocabulary lesson. "I'll tell you later," she said through clinched teeth.

"Well, the good news is the intruder didn't get the envelope," Rani said.

"You're right, Rani," Lanny said. "But we don't know if the person had time to read the letter and the puzzle poem or if those items were even what they came here for."

Lexi was often exasperated by her brother's logical thinking, but she knew his clarity of thought and demand for hard evidence were what made him the head of The Botanic Hill Detectives Agency and the main person responsible for their recently-earned success as amateur investigators.

"Well, I suggest we go back downstairs," Isabela said. "I'd like to hear what you make of my great-grandfather's puzzle poem." She held it up while motioning the kids toward the door.

"Awesome," Lexi replied as she almost galloped into the hallway. The mystery was in full gear now!

CHAPTER FOUR

· ✧ ·

The Puzzle Poem

Everyone was quiet and deep in thought as they descended to the first floor and headed once again for the living room. This case was serious. A million-dollar gem was somewhere in this house, and there was an intruder lurking around, probably searching too. With that much at stake, would the intruder resort to something worse than simply stomping and scaring? Lanny had argued at the top of the stairs that it didn't seem likely since surely something bad would have happened by now. But it still gave them the creeps.

Moki was at the back of the line. As he stepped off the last stair, his foot slipped on the small area rug in the entryway. He caught himself using the banister, a startled cry blurting from his lips.

The rug ended up in a heap a few yards away.

"Are you all right?" Isabela asked while trying to help him. "Please be very careful around here, Moki. My grandmother, Ana Sophia, made that rug. And this floor is slippery."

Moki nodded with a red face as he bent to straighten the rug. "Slippery is right."

Isabela helped and said, "I am glad you're all right."

"I'll try to be more careful, Ms. de Cordoba. Sorry. I can be a klutz sometimes." Moki's words far from soothed her. Lexi read the look on Isabela's face. Instead of sympathy this time, the girl gave Moki a huge frown.

Once in the living room, all the kids crowded around Isabela on the sofa to hear the puzzle poem. It was written on a single sheet of crisp yellowed paper in beautiful cursive handwriting. The blue ink was slightly faded but, fortunately, still readable.

"Here is what it says," said Isabela. "I'll be curious if you can make any sense out of it." She smoothed the crinkled sheets and began to read:

"Wishful dreams of bold emerald trappings
From radiant treetop and archaic wrappings;
To find what you seek, you must dash and dart
Only to discover the ending was at the start.

Deep down below a chamber to nourish
The players' voices, where still flourish
Wooden words helped create the magic:
Sometimes comic and sometimes tragic.

Lions' threatening stares from their moonlit perches
Warn of danger for would-be explorers' searches;
But once their eyes are turned down to the floor,

The way becomes clear, it reveals much more.

An artisan's tilework leads to loftier places
Where there are myriad quarters with timeworn traces.
When the sunlight's ray strikes the portrait at three,
Look to the jeweled hand that recommends your knee.

Treehouse gardens seen from highest window stained,
Its panes have witnessed material treasures that remain
Dazzling and fine, but now hidden, soon forgotten with time,
Perhaps to be rescued because of this rhyme.

At the end of it all, blackened roses, wicked thorns, and
 delusions,
So from Gray's elegy, I ask if beauty isn't wasted in
 seclusion?
Searching must continue now but at a funeral's pace,
 awaiting the light
That appears however improbably, yet shining green and
 eternally bright."

She lowered the poem to her lap and looked at the four thirteen-year-olds, whose eyes were glazed over, and whose mouths without exception were open in amazement.

After a moment, Lexi said, "I repeat. He sure had a way with words."

Rani smiled. "What an incredibly talented man—first an actor, then a poet."

"Uh, guys," Moki said. "I hate to interrupt your admiration society, but we really have our work cut out for us here."

Lanny was alert to the quaver in Moki's voice. "Right, Moki, but I'm already making some sense out of the poem," his best friend said as he reached for the page in Isabela's outstretched hand.

Moki said, "You know, Lanny, I never thought I'd admit this in a million years, but I'm glad you're so smart." He let his head drop and wiped his brow with the back of his hand. His sense of timing was everything. Everyone in the room stopped holding their breath and laughed. Moki, too.

"Thanks, bro, but you're right about us having lots of work to do. For starters, this puzzle, or treasure map for the hunt, will take us all over the house and maybe beyond. It's pretty broad. Boy, there's a lot here." He studied the poem and bit his lower lip.

Lexi leaned toward the poem and pointed to the first word. "Yes, I see what you mean. Let's start with the facts. Pick out the nouns first, like 'treetop,' 'chamber,' 'deep down below,' 'lions' and 'perches,' 'tilework,' 'portrait' and 'hand,' and so on. Those sound like specific things or places we can locate, then investigate."

"Poetry and song lyrics, that's our Lexi," Rani said.

Isabela sighed with relief. "I knew bringing you kids in was a good idea. We'll find the emerald for sure now. And I want to try to locate its legal owner. I have no interest in its value for myself or my family. We've all been blessed with everything we could ever need. If no other legal owner is found, I will donate it to charity."

Lexi smiled. "Then you and your great-grandfather are thinking along the same lines."

"It certainly sounds that way. Must be because we're related." Isabela laughed.

They huddled around the poem for a moment in silence. A grandfather clock ticking in the background and the rain still tapping at the windows and patio were now more obvious.

Then, Isabela stretched her arms upward and stifled a yawn. "Is anyone else getting really sleepy? I suggest all of us head to our beds and take this up in earnest in the morning. Maybe the sun will return by then to help shed more light on everything, literally. And I'm so grateful you're all here."

"Thanks," Rani said. "We're glad we're here, too. But do you have a safe place where the letter and poem can be stored overnight? That intruder might return. We don't want to lose those documents."

"Good thinking, Rani. Right here behind this picture frame is our family's wall safe. I'll lock them up immediately. And Lanny, I can see the question on your face. 'Does anyone else know the safe's combination?' The answer is no, just my brother and I, and he's up in Los Angeles interning at an architectural firm for a few more days." She placed the letter and poem inside, closed the door, twirled the lock, and re-covered the safe with the artwork.

Then Isabela stirred the embers in the fireplace and snuffed out all the living room candles. The four kids fanned out room to room downstairs, making sure all the doors and windows were locked. Ten minutes later, the five friends wearily pulled themselves up the stairs, hands on the banister, staggering where they had easily sprinted up earlier in the evening.

"Which bedrooms do you kids want? You may each have your own if you like," Isabela said. "There are eight on this floor. I'm going to change rooms tonight in case the intruder returns."

"Well, to be honest, Ms. de Cordoba, all our parents were nervous about letting us stay here overnight after you told them about the strange noises," Lexi said. "But they agreed it would be all right as long as we stuck together."

"That's right, BFF," Rani said. "So, you and I should share a room."

"And Lanny and I will do the same," Moki said quickly. He received a hoped-for nod from Lanny, who nonetheless rolled his eyes at this parental intrusion.

"Chicken," Lanny said.

"Bawk, bawk!" Moki replied while flapping his curled-up arms like wings. The others laughed. Moki could always be counted on to keep things light, especially when they needed it most.

The kids quickly chose their two rooms, goodnights were said all around, and lights were turned out. Soon, everyone settled down to a long sleep with the wind and the rain still hammering outside.

That is, until the crash at four a.m.

CHAPTER FIVE

· ✧ ·

A Rude Awakening

Lexi and Rani were the first two to grab their robes, shuffle into their slippers, and scramble out into the hallway. Within seconds, the boys were there, flashlights beaming, also trying to process the loud crash.

"What the heck was that?" Lexi asked. Her green eyes glowed wildly as she scanned the hall. She was gripping Rani's arm so hard that her friend finally gave a little cry. Squeezing people's arms when she was scared or excited was Lexi's bad habit.

Isabela joined them, swaddled in a luxurious, long pink robe. She looked just as startled as they were.

Moki rubbed the sleep from his eyes. "Sounded as if maybe Big Foot returned, this time wearing the world's heaviest army boots."

Isabela said, "I'm pretty sure it came from outside. Come with me." She flipped on the hall lights, then led them at a run down the entire length of the hall to the twisting staircase leading to the third floor. She paused there and said, "There's a solarium upstairs with a perfect view of the back gardens."

When they reached the room and approached the floor-to-ceiling window that spanned the length of the solarium, Isabela flicked a switch. A substantial area of the yard was flooded with light. They were all shocked at what they could see despite the raging storm. Two tall, mature eucalyptus trees had crashed to the ground, their black roots now exposed. As they fell, they had apparently toppled another tree farther out in the yard. The first two had just missed the swimming pool and patio furniture, but it wasn't clear whether or not a small building beyond the third tree had been hit.

"There could be more trees down from the storm," Isabela said. "We'll have to wait until sunrise to make a full inspection. No sense in going out there now in the dark, rain, and mud. I doubt anyone was injured or electric wires or phone lines brought down."

"'Anyone'?" Lanny asked. "Is someone else on your property?"

"Yes, I have a tenant in the caretaker's old *casita*— 'cottage'—at the far end of the flower garden, near that third downed tree. She's elderly and never leaves the *casita* in bad weather, but I'm going to call and check on her, anyway." Isabela excused herself, pulled her cell phone from her robe pocket, and walked away from the huge window to make the call.

"Ms. de Cordoba, what a cool room to watch a storm from or just check out the gardens," Moki said. But Lexi put her finger to her lips.

She glanced toward Isabela, who was currently standing with her back to them, and whispered, "Cool it, Moki. Can't you see that Ms. de Cordoba's trying to call someone?"

The kids couldn't help but catch bits of the one-sided conversation. "Oh, thank goodness you're all right, Madame Ronescu. . . . No damage? . . . And Oso, is he still there with you? . . . Great. Thanks. Sorry to have disturbed you. I'll come see both of you in a few hours. Goodnight."

The kids' questioning expressions were not lost on Isabela as she faced them. She wasted no time in explaining. "Madame Ronescu is from Europe. She and my cousin Olivia became friends there. Olivia sent a letter with the woman a couple of months ago suggesting I rent the old *casita* to her during her extended stay in the United States. She seemed friendly then, so I agreed. As to Oso, he's my sweet, lovable, lazy eight-year-old basset hound baby who thinks the *casita* is his doghouse."

"You have a dog?" Rani asked. "Dogs can be great for protecting people and property."

"Yes. Come to think of it, Oso has been doing some extra sniffing around rooms lately."

"Where?" Lexi asked. She hugged herself to ward off the chill in the glassed-in room.

"Mostly around the walls all over the house."

The kids' eyebrows hiked.

Lanny smiled broadly. "That could give us a valuable lead, Ms. de Cordoba."

Isabela said, "Great. I'm glad Oso might be able to help. So now, what's it going to be? Back to bed, or to the kitchen for some Mexican hot chocolate? We could get better acquainted, waiting for the sunrise. And I've never heard the intruder this early in the morning, so I doubt you'll be missing out on any investigating." She sounded perky even though she was still hugging herself with anxiety.

Rani's large brown eyes lit up. "I'm always ready for chocolate in any form, plus conversation."

"We can sleep anytime," Lanny said. "I was awake listening for the intruder, anyway."

"Maybe some cinnamon toast to go with that hot chocolate?" Moki the foodie asked.

"Moki, you're so predictable," Lexi said, gently punching the boy's muscular arm.

"Predictable and well fed. That's how I like it." He led the way downstairs.

After checking that the letter and poem were still secure in the living room wall safe, the group headed for the kitchen. Isabela prepared the hot chocolate with a dash of its secret ingredient, cayenne pepper. Moki slathered toast with gobs of butter and heavy shakes of cinnamon-sugar. Soon, everyone settled onto high stools around the cooking island to eat, talk, and await the sunrise.

Isabela finished a sip from her mug. "I'm curious. It's

September. Why aren't you kids in school? Oh, don't get me wrong. I'm not complaining. I'm very glad you're here."

"Thanks. Lexi and I are homeschooled," Lanny replied after wiping his mouth with his napkin. "We have a tutor named Bruce Wilding, who actually lives in our house. He's twenty-five and has a teaching credential."

"Yeah," Lexi yawned. "Our mom is an art historian, and our dad is an archaeologist. They work at the ARC— the Antiquities Research Collective—and are often sent by the director, Dr. Leland Abbott, on assignments around the world. Having a tutor lets us all travel together and not miss our 'book learning,' as Bruce calls it."

Moki said, "When they travel, Rani and I usually go with them. My dad and Rani's parents get work from our teachers at Las Palmitas Middle School, and Bruce teaches us, too. That includes when we're on a case here in town, like now." The boy stuffed half a slice of toast into his mouth.

"We accidentally solved a mystery in Paris, France, last year," Rani said. Seeing the puzzled look on Isabela's face, she continued, "It wasn't an official case. I mean we didn't know the thieves would crash into us and spill their loot out onto the sidewalk as we walked past a jewelry store."

"As a result, you helped the police catch those diamonds thieves, yes?" asked Isabela.

Moki buffed this fingernails. "Yeah. And it went viral on social media."

"I remember that. It's why I knew you could help me." Isabela sipped at her cocoa. "Amazing, to have a proven track record of success at your young age, even if it was by accident. But you also helped Mrs. Thornsley over on Nutmeg Street by solving that case involving the stolen Egyptian urn." Her smiled widened as she gazed at the kids. "I know Moki's dad is with the Las Palmitas Police Department. What do your parents do, Rani?"

"Well, my dad is a geology professor at the university. My mom is a manager for Far Horizons Airlines. She works at the airport."

"Yeah, and we love listening to Mrs. Kumar's interesting airport stories," Lexi said. "Like the time she had Johnny Depp and his bodyguard in her private office to protect them from a mob of crazy fans."

"Wow. Now, that's very interesting, indeed," replied Isabela, "especially since 'Captain Jack Sparrow' is one of my favorite actors."

"Arrgh!" Moki said in his best pirate voice. "You know, people tell me that I'm his Hawaiian twin."

Lanny replied, "Maybe, dude—in your dreams. I mean, you're missing the moustache. And there isn't even any hair above your upper lip yet. Not to mention you also lack acting talent, bro."

"Oh, I don't know," Lexi replied. "Moki's quite handsome . . . and a ham."

He gave her a wink. "Being Hawaiian, I'd have to say Spam, not ham."

Isabela smiled at the kids' banter and turned to Rani. "I meant to compliment you on your tattoos. Henna, yes?" Rani's hands and arms were decorated with reddish-brown designs that showed up well on her dark skin. "Did you do them yourself? What are the chances I can convince you to do some on me?"

"Yes, I did, and pretty good on the chances," Rani replied. "We can pick out designs and colors later."

Isabela nodded her head slowly. "You know, you're all certainly so kind, smart, and mature for your age. How fortunate for me that you are my neighbors."

Lexi replied for the squad. "Thanks. All our parents raised us to be responsible and polite. And because we're lucky to have so much, we should 'pay it forward.'"

Lanny added, "Becoming detectives taught us something, too. That if we aren't smart and mature, people won't ask for our help. And we *want* to help people."

Moki said, "Since my dad's a police officer, he says I especially need to set a good example for the community. Sometimes, it's hard to live up to that, but I try."

"Well, I'd say you're succeeding quite nicely," Isabela said. Moki beamed.

"Growing up in a Latinx and European family taught me to love and respect adults. In my case, those adults were my parents and teachers. Rani, I imagine you were raised in a similar way, being from India."

Rani said, "Yes. Children in India are taught to be obedient and respectful toward their parents and other

EUCALYPTUS STREET: GREEN CURSE

adults and to take care of them as they get older. My grandma lives with us here. I love it! She's so much fun. Plus, she helps since both my parents work."

"Rani's lucky," said Lexi. "I wish my grandparents lived with us. But Nana and Papa Marlton live in England. And Grams and Poppy Wyatt are in Chicago. We don't get to see any of them very often."

Lexi quickly glanced at her bestie. "There's something else you should know about Rani, Ms. de Cordoba."

Rani's dark eyebrows knitted together. "There is? Like what?" She tilted her head and awaited the answer.

"You know! Your synesthesia," Lexi said. She explained to Ms. de Cordoba, "That means Rani can taste things when certain words are said."

"Really? That's fascinating, Rani," Isabela said. "I've heard of synesthesia but never knew anyone who had it—that is, until now."

"It's true," Rani said. "I recently discovered I am a synesthete. The condition is considered an ability, not a disability, and it's rare. Synesthesia occurs when someone is born with extra connections in their brain between usually unrelated senses. In my case, hearing and tasting. I hear a word or a name, and I actually taste something. For example, 'Lexi' is pretzels. 'Lanny' is sweet potatoes. 'Moki' is blueberry pie with ice cream. And 'Rani' is raw green beans—but sometimes, it's the white part of the watermelon rind. But I don't have a clue why it changes tastes."

"Wow. Okay, I have to ask. What's 'Isabela'?"

"Potato chips. Very salty, thick, crinkle-cut potato chips to be exact."

Everyone laughed except Rani, who only smiled. She understood how novel this concept must seem for anyone except herself or other synesthetes.

Moki said, "I think Rani's synesthesia could somehow help us solve mysteries."

"I doubt it could, Moki," Rani replied, "but it would be fun if that happened."

Lanny, always a stickler for logic and facts, merely frowned.

All at once, the kitchen was lit up by a beautiful pink and orange sunrise. Rays passed through a few leftover storm clouds in the eastern sky, then glinted off the kitchen cupboards.

"Hey, the rain has finally stopped!" said Isabela. She glanced at the wall clock. "Well, time flies when there's interesting conversation."

"And when there's good food," Moki said as he finished his fourth piece of toast.

"We'll have a real breakfast in a couple of hours when my cook, Tina, arrives from town. Will you really be hungry by then, Moki?"

"He'll be hungry!" the other three kids shouted together.

Moki gave two thumbs up amid much laughter.

"Well, okay then. It was wonderful getting to know

all of you better. Now, let's get dressed and meet on the back patio in twenty minutes," Isabela said. "Time to explore."

At last, the storm damage inspection was about to begin. And something told Moki that it was important for them to meet Madame Ronescu. The sooner, the better.

CHAPTER SIX

· ✧ ·

At the Root of It All

A short time later, the kids were assembled on the patio with Isabela as instructed. They were prepared with hiking boots on and pant legs rolled up, ready to challenge the soggy, muddy lawns. No sari for Rani today. She knew their muddy exploration called for a pair of sturdy old jeans.

Lanny scanned the far horizon with a hand shielding his eyes. "Just how large is your property, Ms. de Cordoba? It takes up about three city blocks, doesn't it? The wrought-iron fence seems to go on forever."

"Yes. The property is about six acres now. It used to be larger until my grandparents sold part of our land to St. Barnabas Catholic Cathedral."

They all knew the church well. It was a fixture in the neighborhood, bordering the western edge of the de Cordoba estate.

Moki cast his eyes over the scene. "Looks like a national park to me or about six football fields. Yeah, we'll definitely be busy for the next few hours. Glad I ate all that cinnamon toast."

"I'm sure you'd be glad you ate it even if we weren't going to be busy," Lexi said. She smiled up sweetly at the self-proclaimed Hawaiian version of Johnny Depp.

"Well, let's get started," Isabela said before Moki could respond. She set out for the closest fallen trees. "Still a little windy. Watch out for mud puddles." The four kids looked like rabbits, hopping after the woman in a single-file line, trying to step where she had just walked.

They passed the huge, colorfully-tiled swimming pool with chaise lounges scattered about. Lanny had visions of it in its heyday with Lorenzo and Alondra's actor and actress friends down from Hollywood for weekends. They would have been swimming or lounging, working on their tans to look their best in front of the cameras come Monday. *Wow. That was ages ago*, he mused.

Everyone was disheartened at the site of the old, fallen eucalyptus trees. They had been magnificent. Now, their spindly black roots were exposed, projecting like enormous craggy spider legs in all directions. Their trunks and branches were in a tangled, undignified heap.

Isabela sighed. "I'm just sick about losing these trees. Tomás, Olivia, and I had a homemade swing attached to the lowest branch of that one." She pointed to a nearby tree. "It gave us many memorable hours of fun as kids. Well, another loss. Those shallow roots and the storm are to blame. I'll have to call my tree people and the gardeners to come help with this mess after we've assessed all the damage." Her voice almost cracked.

"Looks like a major clean-up chore, all right," Lanny said. He lifted a heavy branch, then set it down gently to show respect for the dead. Moki and Lexi also grew quiet, mainly for Isabela's sake, as if attending a dear friend's funeral.

Sharp-eyed Rani had wandered off as usual. She had been circling the two trees, staring at the ground underneath them.

"Guys, come here. What do you make of this?"

Everyone snapped to attention and gathered around her. They tried to look down between the boughs, expecting to see shallow holes where the toppled trees had churned up the ground. But the holes were deep.

Lanny said, "It looks like a brick-lined cavern down there." He tried to climb inside.

"Hold it right there, Lanny," Isabela ordered, and the boy froze. "I'm very curious, too, but that ground is soggy and possibly unstable after the storm. You could be buried in mud. You'll need to wait until I can get the gardeners here to clear the debris and shore things up. Sorry to delay your investigation, but I think your parents would agree with my taking these precautions."

"I'm just as curious as you and Lanny are," Moki said, "but I have to side with you, Ms. de Cordoba. Plus, I had planned on staying clean at least until after breakfast."

Lexi said, "Hey, Ms. de Cordoba, good going. You

appealed to my brother's extreme sense of logic. If there's one thing Lanny responses to, it's logic. Eh, Mr. Sherlock Holmes?" She feigned a British accent.

"Someone has to be logical, and I'm the most qualified," Lanny said. He scrunched up his face at his sister.

Despite the jokes, all four kids really were reluctant to put the muddy mystery on hold. They slowed their pace considerably in the hope that Isabela would change her mind. Their strategy failed.

"Okay, so, we're all agreed. No exploring around here until I give the go-ahead, yes?"

Following weak nods from the kids, Isabela continued, "Now, let's check out the third fallen tree, the flower garden, and the *casita*. I'm anxious to see how Madame Ronescu and Oso are." She, too, glanced over her shoulder at the mysterious, deep holes as they walked on.

Lanny noticed the woman's curiosity. "Ms. de Cordoba, if there's one cavern, there might be more. In fact, this whole area might be honeycombed with them."

She stopped and faced him. "That's exactly what I was thinking, Lanny. If so, this ground might be unstable and on the verge of collapse. I better have an engineer come assess the area, too. I'm afraid that activity could further delay your investigating it on your own, but I think it's necessary."

"I'm sure my dad can help by bringing some of his geologist's tools if you'd like him to come over and check things out," Rani said.

"And I know my dad, the archaeologist, would help, too," Lexi said.

"Perfect!"

The group moved on to the exotic flower garden. Most of the hibiscus bushes and bird-of-paradise plants were soggy and windblown but otherwise fine. The dozen or so mature dragon trees had also survived. Turning the next corner, they saw a third fallen eucalyptus tree, the largest of the three, and the caretaker's *casita*. Their mouths dropped open.

"Wow, close call," Rani said. "That eucalyptus tree barely missed the side of the cottage."

"Thank goodness. A very close call, indeed," Isabela replied.

A sizable branch lay less than four feet from the side of the old place. The only damage seemed to be that a decorative window shutter had apparently been blown off and was now lying on its side against the building.

Before they had knocked on the door, loud, deep barking could be heard coming from inside the little house. As the door creaked open slowly, out plodded Isabela's milk-chocolate-color dog.

"Oso, you big baby," Isabela said. She stooped down to play with his ears and pet him vigorously. His sturdy tail wagged at lightning speed, and he initially ignored the four kids in favor of his owner's affection. "I really missed you during the storm, but I knew you were okay."

"Aww," said Rani and Lexi. The two were on their

knees despite the wet grass. They had never met a dog they didn't like. Oso lumbered over to them with his low, heavy body, ready to make new friends.

"*Oso* is Spanish for 'bear,' isn't it?" Lexi asked.

Isabela replied, "That's right, Lexi. When I first got him, I thought he looked like a little brown bear cub. That's how he got his name."

The girls were so distracted by the dog that they were entirely caught off-guard by the sound of a deep voice rasping from behind the cottage door.

It slowly opened just a crack more. "Who's there?"

CHAPTER SEVEN

· ✧ ·

Casita, Cathedral, and Cemetery

An elderly woman, cane in hand, slowly emerged from the dark house. She was stooped over and about eighty years old. Her face looked like a shriveled peach. She was dressed in a well-worn, long gathered cotton skirt made from many yards of purple calico fabric. A tattered black shawl was wrapped around her shoulders, and her raggedy gingham head scarf was so large, it allowed only wisps of wiry gray hair to show. Golden hoop earrings hung heavily, distending her pierced earlobes, and many bangles encircled both wrists. A shiny gold coin necklace almost covered some stains on her beige blouse. The strong smells of herbs, cabbage, and garlic emanated from the kitchen stove at the back of the place.

"Hello, Madame Ronescu," Isabela said, smiling at the woman.

The tenant looked her landlady up and down through dark, squinting eyes. "Well?"

Isabela ignored the rudeness. "As I said on the phone, I'm so glad you survived the storm. And thanks for looking after Oso. I'd like you to meet my new friends."

She introduced each of the children by name. Madame Ronescu mostly grunted in reply and appeared uncomfortable about being touched. After she rebuffed Lanny's handshake, the other kids didn't bother to try. Lexi for one was glad. The woman's hands looked oily from cooking.

"You have an interesting accent," Rani said. "May I ask where you're from?"

"I am visiting here from my faraway homeland of Romania," she said in a deep monotone.

"That is far away. Why did you decide to come all the way to California, Madame Ronescu?" Lexi asked. She couldn't help but gawk at the woman's heavily made-up, wrinkled face and expensive-looking jewelry.

"I came for the sun. I hope we get some soon," was her level reply. Her penetrating, intense stare made Lexi a bit uneasy, as if she were being hypnotized against her will.

Isabela did a quick inspection inside the *casita*. When she found no damage, the group said their good-byes to the old woman, who disappeared inside and slammed the door decisively in their faces. Isabela ignored her and continued their walk. Oso gladly loped after his owner as the group resumed inspecting the grounds.

Once Isabela was far out in front of them, Moki

whispered to Lexi, "Madame Ronescu 'came for the sun'?" He glanced back toward the building. "Looks more like she came for the shadows . . . and the dark, and the full moon, and flying bats, and howling wolves, and—"

"Except vampires don't eat garlic, Moki," Lexi said, her eyebrows pinched together.

"Oh, yeah, right. I forgot about that. But she still sounds like Countess Dracula to me. In fact, just thinking about her makes my neck hurt. Bet there aren't any mirrors inside her cottage. And she must be cramped in there, being used to living in a huge old European, ancestral castle."

"You know, I thought I had an active imagination," Lexi said, "but you've got me beat." She quickened her step to catch up with Lanny and Rani. Moki followed her, not wanting to be left behind.

"Hey, Rani," Moki called. "What does 'Madame Ronescu' make you taste?" He truly believed Rani's synesthesia could give them valuable clues.

"You don't want to know." Rani scrunched up her nose and frantically waved both hands in front of her face for air. Lanny had slowed down to rejoin the squad.

"Ha! That proves what I was saying about—"

Lexi shook her head. "Oh, Moki. Get real. This is California, not Castle Dracula."

"Madame Ronescu looks like a Gypsy, but way over the top," Lanny said to his friends.

"The more respectful term is 'Rom' or 'Roma,' not

'Gypsy,'" Rani said. "The Roma come from India, Macedonia, Romania, and Spain, and have the Romany language in common. They are a hard-working, fun-loving people who have too often been the victims of stereo-typing." The squad could count on Rani for teaching them to respect other cultures.

"I still say something's not right," Lanny said. "And she certainly isn't 'fun-loving.'"

"And I still say watch your necks," Moki replied, grasping his with both hands.

"What happened to fairness and hard evidence?" Rani asked. Everyone became quiet.

The four kids caught up with Isabela, who had stopped short. "That's unfortunate," she said. Then, she pointed to the edge of the property. "The whole area over there looks as if it's been badly damaged."

She ran toward it with the kids and Oso lumbering behind her. There had been an enormous patch of daisies that skirted the entire length of a low stone wall. What remained were bits of white and yellow petals with stems and leaves crushed into the soil.

"I can't blame this on the wind or rain," Isabela said. She squatted to lift some of the dead flowers. "From the looks of things, I'd say this bed was trampled by humans or animals."

Oso gave a little yelp. "No, not you, big baby," Isabela said. "You know better." The dog started intently sniffing the flower bed.

Lanny kneeled down to examine the spot. "Is this an area that normally gets a lot of foot traffic?"

"I don't think so," Isabela replied. "It doesn't make sense. It's not out in the open. Well, add this to your list of mysteries to solve here at the *casa*, kids."

"Looks like the work of Big Foot to me," Lexi said.

Lanny grinned, never too confident in his sister's often rushed theories. He added the trampled flowers to his mental list of mysteries to solve on this case. The four kids inspected the area but found nothing else out of the ordinary.

"This brings us to the churchyard of St. Barnabas Cathedral," Isabela said. Like a tour guide, she extended her hand, palm up, toward the building and its grounds. "That low stone wall, now minus the daisies, separates the de Cordoba property from that of the cathedral."

The building was mammoth and a stunning replica of European Gothic architecture. Ivy growing profusely on some of its pointed exterior arches, ribbed vaults, and flying buttresses indicated the building had been part of the community for many years. Circular rose windows and tall lancet-shaped stained-glass windows dominated the beige stucco walls every few feet. For now, the kids could only imagine how beautiful the interior must look when sunlight permeated the colorful glass mosaics.

After staring up at the building for a full minute, Moki felt dizzy and shook his head. "So, what kinds of things are planted in a churchyard?" he asked casually.

"Dead bodies, old buddy," Lanny replied, not missing a beat.

Moki stopped abruptly in his tracks, looked down at the headstones across the stone wall, and started coughing. Lanny slapped him on the back, and everyone else chuckled.

Dense foliage from pine, magnolia, and jacaranda trees could not obscure a colossal white marble building that looked like a Grecian temple a short distance inside the wall. It appeared windowless and had three long, low steps leading up to a black wrought iron door. The name "de Cordoba" was emblazoned across the pediment in gold letters, which sparkled despite the area being merely dappled with sunlight. Its entry was flanked by two massive, carved marble angels on pedestals. Isabela noticed the kids looking at the structure quizzically.

"That's my family's mausoleum," she said softly. "My parents, grandparents, great-grandparents, and great-great-grandparents are buried inside. Some relatives from Olivia's side of the family rest there as well. This is the section of the church property we used to own. It was sold in the 1970s so the church could create a holy burial ground for its parishioners." She made the sign of the cross on herself and blew a gentle kiss toward her ancestors' resting place.

Changing the subject slightly, Isabela said, "The pastor of St. Barnabas is Monsignor Peter Connolly, but he prefers to be called Father Pete. He's very easygoing and friendly. If you find yourselves over this way, I'm sure he'd be more than happy to help you, even give you a tour of the cathedral. It's very beautiful inside. He lives around the corner in the rectory, the priests' residence, on the west side of the building."

"Are we allowed to enter the churchyard right now?" Rani asked in a hushed tone.

"Of course," Isabela said. She led the group through the small gate in the stone wall.

As they walked toward the enormous burial chamber, Moki hung back a bit, eyeing the numerous old and new headstones. Pine needles crunched under everyone's feet. Lexi and Rani stopped three times to look at the names and dates on some of the headstones. They noted one was for an infant who, if still alive, would be forty years old now.

Lanny slowed down to join his friend. "You okay, bro?"

"Well, sure, but let's put it this way. I'd rather be in Disneyland. And I wish we hadn't met Madame Ronescu after all."

"Okay, it's your turn to teach me a word. How do you say 'chicken' in Hawaiian?" Lanny dodged a friendly cuff to the head from his best friend, and the two soon caught up with the others by the de Cordoba mausoleum.

The eastern side wall of the cathedral was a few yards away. Some of last spring's faded purple blossoms from the nearby giant jacaranda tree still littered the ground around the building. A crow cawed, and a small airplane buzzed far overhead. Otherwise, the cemetery was silent and empty. Even Oso sat respectfully still, watching his owner for a cue.

Isabela ambled toward her family's mausoleum but stopped at the bottom step. The kids noticed the puzzled look that spread across her face.

"Now that's odd," she said. "I left a bouquet of flowers on these steps on my birthday to honor my family as I do every year. Hmm, the storm must have blown it away."

CHAPTER EIGHT

· ✧ ·

Mud and More Paper

A shriek came from the kitchen. "Oh no you don't!"
Isabela and her four guests were seated at the
dining room table after their morning inspection of the
gardens and the cemetery. They instantly dropped their forks
and spoons, left their delicious brunch, and raced to the
kitchen. There they found Tina the cook holding Oso by
his collar, trying to prevent him from taking another step.

"What's happening?" Isabela asked the tall, sturdy,
middle-aged woman.

"Oh ma'am, I'm so sorry to have disturbed you and
your company, but Oso has tracked quite a lot of mud
across the kitchen floor. I was trying to keep him here, so I
could wipe off his paws before he reached the carpets."

Isabela exhaled in relief. "No need to apologize,
Tina. You did the right thing. Yes, please clean him up if
you don't mind. I should have done that myself when we
returned from our garden tour."

The group went back to the dining room to finish their meal. They had just gotten reseated when Lanny said, "Ms. Tina and Oso just made me think of something. Last night when that intruder was here, why didn't we find any wet, muddy footprints on the carpets upstairs?"

Rani almost dropped her fork onto her plate again. "That's right, Lanny. It was pouring outside, but you'd never have known it from the clean, dry carpets."

"I still think Big Foot has a secret way in and out of the house," Lexi said, "and not by the usual windows or doors." She finished her last swallow of orange juice.

"Lexi makes sense," Moki said. He winked at Lexi as he reached for more bacon. "Bigfoot maybe came in by a longer route. That let his or her feet dry off, and the mud get scraped off first."

Isabela paused, held her coffee cup in midair, and said, "Yes. And remember I mentioned that no alarms have been triggered, yet an intruder seems to gain access to my home? Hmm . . . sounds to me like this old house might have some secret passageways or hidden rooms! What do you kids think?"

"I think you're on to something," Lanny said for the squad. "Just as big houses and castles sometimes did in those old Hollywood mystery and horror movies."

Isabela's eyes shone like crystals. "That's right, and with my great-grandparents being Hollywood actors, maybe they got inspired by those films to add hidden rooms or passageways for some reason. What an intriguing idea."

She rested her chin on one hand. "We need my brother, Tomás, here."

Rani devoured a chunk of cantaloupe. "How can he help us?"

"He has the blueprints for this house. Tomás was working with an out-of-town architectural firm during the summer because he wants to become an architect after college. He loves old houses. He might know about possible secret passageways here."

"That reminds me," Lanny said. "In old Hollywood, there was another famous silent movie star who lived next door to an equally famous movie director. They became good friends and had a tunnel dug to connect their houses. That way, they could visit each other without having to go outside where they might be mobbed by fans and photographers. Back then, not all celebrities' properties were fenced or guarded as many are today."

"How fascinating, Lanny," Isabela replied. "Who were the two celebrities?"

Before Lanny could answer, the doorbell rang. Oso, with newly cleaned paws, came galloping through the dining room at an unusually fast pace and headed for the front entry.

"Funny. I'm not expecting anyone," Isabela said. She excused herself, set her napkin on the table, and followed the dog to see who was at the door.

"Ooh Lanny," Rani said. "Your story about the

EUCALYPTUS STREET: GREEN CURSE

Hollywood tunnel! Could that be what that cavern in the backyard is?"

Lanny's gaze slowly met Rani's. "You know, maybe . . ."

Moki forcefully slammed his hand down upon the table, rattling the silverware. "Darn. If only we could go investigate it right now."

"Does that mean you've had enough to eat and are ready to get dirty?" Lexi teased.

"I don't think I've ever in my life used the phrase, 'I've had enough to eat.'"

"Silly me for asking." Lexi rolled her eyes at Moki for what felt like the millionth time.

Just then, Isabela returned with a handsome man who looked just a little bit older than herself. She introduced him as Mr. Troy Landis from the law office where Lorenzo de Cordoba's letter had been kept for seventy years.

He shook hands with each of them. "I know you kids from your reputation as detectives. Glad to meet you. I'm sure you'll be of immeasurable help to Ms. de Cordoba during your case." He smiled broadly at Isabela.

"Mr. Landis has just brought me another letter in person," Isabela told the kids.

"That's right. Actually, it arrived a year ago from New Delhi, India, inside another envelope. My office has been saving it for you. The instructions on the outer envelope stated you were to receive this only after you had received the letter from your relative, which you did on your birthday. And please, call me Troy."

"Would you please stay, Troy, while I read it?" Isabela asked. "And do call me Isabela."

"My pleasure, Isabela." He joined the group at the table, taking the offered cup of coffee from Tina, but turned down Isabela's invitation to join in breakfast. Rani and Lexi glanced at the lawyer and Isabela, then at each other and smiled. Sparks between two people so obviously attracted to one another always grabbed the girls' attention.

"It's addressed to 'A Relative of Lorenzo de Cordoba' in care of the law firm," she began. "I wonder how the writer knew to send it there. It's from the office of the Indian Minister of Culture."

Mr. Landis shrugged.

She cautiously unfolded two sheets of heavy, expensive-looking paper. The letter was neatly typed.

"It's dated one year ago. Here's what it says:

Dear de Cordoba family relative:

This letter assumes that, by now, you have received a communication from your distant relative, the late Lorenzo de Cordoba, via his attorney.

Former Indian ministers of culture became acquainted with Mr. de Cordoba many years ago when he wrote repeatedly seeking information about a large emerald that was found in our country. He explained the circumstances of how he came to possess it and wondered about its true ownership. My predecessors were unable to help him resolve the matter at that time since no one had reported a stolen or missing emerald.

Your relative revealed he still doubted his legal right to it. He also shared with this office his plan to make the gemstone's whereabouts known to his eldest relative three generations after him via a letter that was to be kept in the vault of his hometown's law firm, Cortez, Jones, Landis and Kent. We didn't want this letter to reach you before your relative's; hence, we sent it directly to the law firm to hold until the appropriate time.

Mr. de Cordoba insisted that if any news about the emerald's ownership surfaced, we were to notify him or the law firm immediately. No information was discovered prior to the gentleman's untimely death in 1965, so neither he nor his attorney was contacted. We are now happy to report, however, that new developments in our investigation have occurred, necessitating this letter.

A team of archaeologists has recently unearthed a large sacred temple in Northern India and plans to restore it. The building had been buried during an earthquake in 1941 and nearly forgotten. Further excavations have revealed the existence of a sacred statue of the chief temple god. It has a large hollow in the center of its forehead. Historical records indicate the statue once housed an enormous faceted emerald in that hollow.

We now believe the emerald in your family's possession came from that statue. If true, it is one of our national treasures. I am enclosing the dimensions and description of the gemstone, based on historical records and drawings.

It is this office's hope, should the emerald be located and determined to belong to the Indian people, that you will return it to us, so we may reunite it with the statue. We trust you will have as strong a sense of justice as did your relative, the honorable Lorenzo de Cordoba.

Please feel free to contact me with questions or if I might assist you with the stone's return.

Yours most sincerely,

Mr. Aadarsh Pandarva,
Indian Minister of Culture, New Delhi

"Isn't that amazing news?" Isabela said. She handed the letter back to Mr. Landis. "That seems to clear up the mystery of the stone's true ownership, at any rate." She glanced at the paper containing the description of the stone.

"It does if your stone is truly the one that came from

the statue," Mr. Landis replied. "The enclosed description will help answer that question once the stone is found. By the way, the 'Landis' mentioned by the Indian official? That's my family. I'm a fourth-generation attorney. My father and grandfather still work at the firm," he said with his head held high.

"So, our two families have been indirectly connected for decades, yes?" Isabela asked.

"That's right. No sense in breaking that connection now as far as I'm concerned." Isabela couldn't help but notice Troy's polite charm.

Yes, definite sparks, Lexi and Rani decided. They did a silent low-five under the table for Isabela.

Lexi recovered herself. "Uh, Ms. de Cordoba, you said you had already decided, like your great-grandfather, that you wanted to find the emerald's legal owner and return it."

Troy leaned toward Isabela. "Is that true?"

She nodded.

He respectfully studied her face and smiled. "That's very generous and kind of you."

Lanny asked Rani, "Do you know anything about the temple Mr. Pandarva mentioned?"

Rani tapped the side of her head. "Not about that specific temple. But I do know what the Indian minister said about temples and statues being sacred is true. I remember seeing lots of gemstones in temple statues when I lived there. Indian people of worship would never remove the stones. That would be disrespectful and a desecration of a shrine."

"Ms. de Cordoba," said Moki with downcast eyes. "How can I say this delicately? Um, it sounds as if your relatives, uh, might have been, um . . . thieves."

"You're possibly right, Moki." She reached over and patted the relieved boy's hand. "All the more reason to right a wrong."

CHAPTER NINE

· ✧ ·

Churchyard on the Third Floor

The next day, after waking up early and preparing their own breakfast, the four kids were planning their day. Once Mr. Landis had left the day before, they spent many hours poring over the puzzle poem. They wanted to continue that work and anxiously waited for Isabela to come downstairs to get the document from the safe. In the meantime, they discussed what they could.

Lexi and Rani loaded their breakfast dishes into the dishwasher. Lexi said, "Seems to me since Alondra's last name was *Luna,* which is Spanish for 'moon,' that might account for the use of 'moonlit perches' in stanza three of the puzzle poem."

"That stanza also includes the word 'lions,'" Lanny replied. He released the handle of the refrigerator where he had just finished putting back the jam jar. "A lion was the symbol of the movie studio where Lorenzo and Alondra made most of their films. Maybe we'll find different kinds of lions to investigate around the house and grounds."

Moki scrubbed the kitchen countertops. "But lions don't sit on perches. Birds do."

"Unless it's a poetic kind of perch," Lexi said. "Not really a perch. Something like a perch. Poets often take liberties with language."

"Say, you guys are way ahead of me," Isabela said as she bounded into the kitchen. "Good morning. Are you losing sleep over the case already?" She reached for a coffee mug from the cupboard.

"When we get on a case, and the ideas start to flow, we can't help but roll with them," Lanny replied. "We hope to continue looking for clues in the puzzle poem today."

Before Isabela could comment on their ambitions, Lexi's cell phone rang. It was the twins' mother, Dr. Rebecca Marlton. Lexi excused herself, as was her habit when she received a call, and headed for the dining room with her phone pressed to her ear.

No sooner had she left when Lanny also got a call. "Ms. de Corboba, it's Dr. Leland Abbott, director of the ARC—you know, where my parents work—in Cortez Park. I better answer it." Taking a cue from his sister, Lanny excused himself, walked into the kitchen's service porch, and closed the door.

"My, but aren't they the popular ones this morning," Moki said. "Well, la-di-da."

"I hope everything's all right," Rani said. She bit

down on her lower lip as she often did when she was nervous.

To pass the time, Moki asked, "Say, Rani, what does the name 'Dr. Abbott' make you taste?" Moki the foodie was especially interested in Rani's synesthetic ability to taste words.

"Cooked apricots with the skins left on—you know, those kind that come in cans."

"Amazing," he said. "I wish I had synesthesia. Maybe I wouldn't be so hungry all the time. It must be an extra treat to be able to taste food without getting all the calories."

Isabela was on her second cup of coffee and amused by Moki for a change. When the twins returned, she asked, "What's up? Any problems?"

Lexi began. "Problem? No, Mom was just reminding us that Aunt Connie arrives late this afternoon from Washington, D.C." Lexi had already explained to Isabela about the twins' aunt, Connie Marlton, a photojournalist with the International Geographic Institute. Dr. Abbott had hired her to photograph his new ARC exhibit, "Gemstones of Antiquity," which would open to the public the next day.

"We're all supposed to go there tonight for the special preview reception. You're invited too, Ms. de Cordoba. Mom also said Bruce wants us four kids to come over today if possible to catch up on some lessons."

"Yay, your aunt Connie is so much fun," said Rani.

She reminded Isabela that her mother worked at the airport, so Mrs. Kumar was happy to meet Ms. Marlton at the arrival gate and drive her to the twins' house.

Lanny had returned, and he looked serious. "Bad news, guys. Dr. Abbott needs our help. When he and the gemstones' curator Mr. Chris Dayton were inspecting the exhibit this morning, they noticed a few of the stones were missing from the display case. The police are investigating, but Dr. A wants us to look into it, too."

"Wow. More missing jewels. Interesting coincidence," Moki said with a faraway look in his eyes.

"Wow is right," Isabela said. Do they think it was a theft, or could the stones have been misplaced?"

"Dr. Abbott and the police are pretty sure it was a theft," Lanny replied. "Mr. Dayton is very upset since he's in charge of safeguarding the exhibit's contents."

"Well, that's important to look into," Isabela said. "So, it sounds as if we all have had an unexpected change of plans. This will be the perfect day, then, for us to separate and get things done. The gardeners and tree people are coming this morning, so I'll be occupied with them. Then, Mr. Landis has invited me to have lunch with him. I also need to run some errands. And Tomás can't get here until tomorrow with our home's blueprints. Those might help you with the puzzle poem and your search for passages. So, you four head off to do what you need to do, and I'll see you tonight at the ARC for the gemstone kick-off party. I'll drive you four back here afterwards."

Lanny smiled and gave Isabela a thumbs up. "Then, we'll see you tonight at the ARC."

"And maybe by tomorrow, we'll finally get to check out that cavern." Moki strained to glance out the kitchen window toward the sunny backyard.

"Ms. de Cordoba, have a great lunch with Mr. Landis," Lexi said. She and Rani couldn't help but snicker.

"Oh I will, girls."

Try as she might, Isabela couldn't hide her blushing cheeks from them.

Four hours of lessons with Bruce in the third-floor classroom at the twins' house on Quince Street left no time to visit Dr. Abbott. They would have to see him that evening. And Aunt Connie hadn't arrived yet.

"So, Bruce, what do you know about a poet named Gray and his elegy?" Lanny asked. "It's related to our current case." He enjoyed testing his tutor's knowledge of obscure information.

"You're referring to Thomas Gray and his poem, 'Elegy Written in a Country Churchyard,'" Bruce replied. "Gray was an eighteenth-century English poet, and his elegy is very famous."

Lanny was convinced Bruce had a library in his head.

"What's an 'elegy'?" Lexi asked. She closed her school books and gave Bruce her full attention. She knew a lot about poetry, but this was a new term, even for her.

"An elegy is a formal poem written as a lament for someone who died in order to honor the person. The word means 'mournful song.' It expresses the poet's thoughts and feelings about the person as well as about death, love, or war. An elegy also has a particular rhyme scheme."

"Why is this one so famous?" Rani asked.

"I can think of a few good reasons, Rani," Bruce replied. "It's beautifully written, and it's one of the stand-out poems from what was called 'The Graveyard School.' Poets of that 'school'—which means a group of similar thinkers or artists—in England and America tried to create through description a liking for gloominess. As if wallowing in sorrow would help poets or the reader get more in touch with the deceased and the poet's message."

Moki sighed. "Sounds gloomy, all right." Then, leaning toward Lanny, he whispered, "Is Bruce always this brilliant?"

Lanny nodded.

"Then, he's forgotten more than I'll ever know."

Bruce added, "Gray's 'Elegy' celebrates the ordinary person, not just heroes or celebrities as some poems do. He talks about how some people die forgotten or without anyone ever knowing what talents they possessed. So, even if they weren't famous, they were still special and should be remembered."

"That's really beautiful," Rani said with a faraway look.

Lanny said, "Kind of like a bright light being hidden

under a bushel basket. It doesn't do any good unless the light can be seen and used."

Lexi replied, "And it seems to explain the line in the puzzle poem that says,

So from Gray's elegy, I ask if beauty isn't wasted in seclusion.

"Maybe the beauty that's being wasted according to Lorenzo is the hidden emerald. Maybe he really *did* want it to be found after all," she said.

"Google the poem, and check it out for yourselves," Bruce said.

Just as the kids were doing that, they heard a shout.

"Surprise!" Aunt Connie and Rani's mother, Gajara Kumar, had sneaked into the classroom. All four kids ran to hug them.

"Well, I should visit more often if this is the kind of welcome I'll get," the twins' aunt said. She laughed as the straps from her leather camera cases slid down her arms.

"Her plane got in a little late, but we're here," Mrs. Kumar said. Her twinkling eyes and bright smile made it impossible for Lexi not to picture Rani all grown up. Mrs. Kumar's and Rani's dozens of bronze bracelets jangled as the two embraced. Rani loved breathing in her mother's sandalwood perfume.

"I can't wait to hear all about the case you're on," Aunt Connie said. "And I guess we're all going to the ARC tonight for a fancy party. Ooh, dress-up time."

Rani smiled. "And you'll finally get to meet Dr. Abbott, the director. He's nice and has a cool English accent. Lexi and I love his fashionable, Euro-style clothes."

"And we'll fill everyone in on our case during dinner," Lexi said, not wanting to let go of her aunt's arm. "Rani's and Moki's parents will be here, plus Bruce, and Uncle Rocky, our cook."

"Hey, greetings, Bruce," Aunt Connie said. She shook his hand, then turned back toward the kids. "I saw Uncle Rocky downstairs. He's whipping up a surprise for our dinner tonight. Mmm." She licked her lips.

"Yeah, then we'll head to the exhibit's kick-off party—" Moki began.

"Which is a good thing," said Lanny, "because Dr. Abbott says there's been some trouble there, and he wants us kids to look into it."

CHAPTER TEN

· ✧ ·

Gemstones of Antiquity

The big evening had arrived. Outside, the ARC was lit up by twirling floodlights shooting skyward, and throngs of people had already gathered out front. The kids and their families were admitted before the general public, so Aunt Connie could meet the director. Plus, the squad needed to get information on the missing gemstones.

Connie Marlton smiled and winked at Rani and Lexi when she saw Dr. Abbott, affirming that he did, indeed, look handsome in his Burberry tuxedo. After the introduction, she got busy photographing the fascinating contents inside the numerous glass display cases and their informative signage.

The kids' parents, Bruce, and Uncle Rocky were strolling and admiring the exhibit along with other ARC employees, their families, and a few city officials, including the mayor and some city council members, all dressed up. Many print and broadcast media were on hand.

"Kids," Dr. Abbott said. "I'd like to introduce you to Mr. Chris Dayton, the curator of the current traveling exhibit, 'Gemstones of Antiquity.' We're pleased to be able to have the stones in town for the next two months." Mr. Dayton appeared every inch a professional gemstone expert in his dark suit, which showed off his height and sandy blond hair.

Lanny agreed with his parents that looking sharp tonight was in order, and his light blue dress shirt with dark pants and a jacket fit right in. He caught Dr. Abbott's approving glance and took the opportunity to ask a question. "Dr. Abbott, do the media or other ARC employees know about the missing gemstones?"

"No, not yet, Lanyon," the director whispered. He seldom used the twins' nicknames. "The police think it best to keep that news quiet until their investigation is further along."

"Which stones are missing, and how did you discover the theft?" Lexi whispered back.

"Well, Alexia, Mr. Dayton has a tally sheet of the stones. He discovered this morning the numbers didn't add up during his count. There are ten missing. As to which stones, let's go over to the display case, and we'll show you where they were." He led the group to a far wall.

Mr. Dayton took up the explanation. "This afternoon after the police left, Dr. Abbott and I re-arranged the stones in the display case to hide the gaps. So far, no one seems the wiser."

In an effort to keep some semblance of festivity in the evening, Dr. Abbott said, "I must say, you two girls look stunning." Rani and Lexi blushed, pleased that their saris were noticed by the highly respected, fashion-conscious director. Rani's pink native costume was complemented by the green one she had loaned to Lexi. Her golden bangles and henna tattoos covered their arms, and they had used some of Mrs. Kumar's sandalwood perfume.

"Hey, what about me?" Moki asked. He looked down at his new Hawaiian shirt.

Dr. Abbott smiled. "Moki, the rebel in you is always refreshing to me."

They had arrived at the glass display case. It was long, rectangular, and well lit. A lock was visible in the back near the top of the case.

"Dr. Abbott, how many people have keys to these cases?" Rani asked.

"Only Mr. Dayton and I," the director said.

Mr. Dayton nodded and then frowned. "You've made me remember something. At the last city where these gemstones were exhibited, my keys went missing for a few hours. I later found them in my coat pocket, but there were no problems at that time, so I didn't think it was important to bring to anyone's attention. It now seems obvious to me someone used them to make a duplicate set."

Lexi said, "And maybe that someone followed you and the exhibit here to Las Palmitas, used the keys, and stole the gems today." Deep creases raked her forehead.

"Maybe that someone is here right now," Moki said. He intended to glance around the room, but his large brown eyes fixated on a platter on the nearby dessert buffet. It was stacked high with chocolate brownies. They were like a magnet to the foodie, and he soon found himself powerless to resist them.

Dr. Abbott looked at the three remaining kids. "Do you think someone would be so bold as to steal the stones, then 'return to the scene of the crime,' as it were?"

"Stranger things have been known to happen, Dr. A," Lanny said. "Is there anyone here you don't know?" Now, as casually as possible, everyone in the group started checking the faces of those in attendance.

At that instant, Dr. Abbott noticed an attractive woman who had just arrived. She looked vaguely familiar to him as she walked toward the group.

Rani waved to her and said, "Dr. Abbott, here comes Isabela de Cordoba who lives on Eucalyptus Street." She admired Isabela in her beautiful short green evening dress covered with sequins.

"Hello, kids," she said with a warm smile and hugged Rani and Lexi. "And you must be Dr. Abbott. The girls have told me so many wonderful things about you." She shook hands with the director. "I can't wait to see the exhibit. I am especially interested in emeralds." She winked at the kids.

Dr. Abbott introduced Mr. Dayton, who led the entire

group to another case with Old World emeralds. As they followed him, Lanny said, "Dr. Abbott, I hope it was all right that we told Ms. de Cordoba about the theft. We were at her house when you called."

"Quite all right, Lanyon. I trust your judgment," the director said. He turned to Isabela. "But Ms. de Cordoba, please keep the information confidential."

The woman nodded her promise.

"You kids were asking which stones are missing," Dr. Abbott said. "It's interesting to me that the emeralds weren't touched. If you read the sign, you'll learn that in ancient Egypt and in many cultures throughout time, emeralds were considered the most valuable gem of all."

"'Valuable' in ancient times didn't mean what it means today," Mr. Dayton added. "Today, we want stones that have shine, sparkle, rarity, and durability. We consider those 'precious.'"

"In other words, *bling*," Lexi said. "Like diamonds— cut, clarity, carat, and color."

"Exactly, Alexia," Dr. Abbott said. "But in ancient times, a gem was valued for its ability to protect the wearer from evil, for its purported healing powers, its symbol of rank and status, or its vivid color, but not its sparkle. In fact, opaque or semi-translucent stones were valued over clear ones. Carnelian, for example, was one of the most precious gems in ancient times, but not today."

Aunt Connie had just joined the group, cameras hanging from her arms. "I was wondering about that. I was expecting sparkling, faceted gems like those we see in jewelry stores today."

Mr. Dayton shrugged. "In ancient times, the technology didn't exist yet to facet and polish diamonds or other gemstones to achieve that brilliant sparkle."

Despite the stones' lack of sparkle, the three kids became mesmerized by them as they went from case to case. Lexi, the future Egyptologist, was impressed with the ages of the stones. She could imagine Queen Cleopatra actually touching or wearing some of these very gems, which gave her goosebumps down her henna-tattooed arms.

Rani interrupted her reverie. "Look, Ms. de Cordoba. The sign over this case says,

Emeralds have remained one of the most prized gemstones from ancient times to today. The Roman emperor Nero used to watch the gladiator matches through a large lens made of emerald because he believed the stone would protect him from going blind in the strong sun."

She giggled softly. "What do you know? The first shades."

Lanny glanced around, then quietly asked, "So, which stones are missing from the cases?"

"Ten of the solid-colored stones. Carnelians, sards, chalcedonies, jaspers, agates, and lapis lazuli," Mr. Dayton said as he pointed to some similar remaining stones for reference.

"The big question I have is why were some stones stolen that aren't considered that valuable by today's standards, and the more expensive ones left behind?" Rani asked.

Moki returned at that moment with a stack of brownies in his hand, minus a plate. But the boy had caught the gist of the conversation.

"Maybe the thief didn't know the difference," he said.

"Maybe the thief is trying to throw us off," Lexi added.

"Maybe the thief isn't finished," Lanny replied.

CHAPTER ELEVEN

· ✧ ·

Down the Cellar Steps

The next day, the squad and Isabela were in her backyard. Eight-foot deep caverns met their stares. The downed trees were gone. A churned-up mess remained. The shift between fancy schmoozing at a museum the night before and slogging around on the edge of muddy holes in the late morning could not be more distinct.

"That's some big pit," Moki said. "If this was Hawai'i, I'd say someone was getting ready for a major luau."

Rani's geologist father, Dr. Devi Kumar, and the twins' archaeologist dad, Dr. Ian Wyatt, had just concluded their investigation of the strange structure.

"This appears to be a hole, not a tunnel," Dr. Kumar said as he rubbed mud from his hands. "The bricks were laid in a circular fashion, and the walls are intact for the most part."

"My guess is this was a cistern or a large fountain when the house was built back in the late nineteenth century," Dr. Wyatt said. He climbed up the ladder to rejoin the kids and Isabela. "There are no other breaks or openings that I could find."

Lexi kicked at the grass and scowled. "Oh, darn. I was hoping for some tunnels and secret passageways under the garden."

"Well, we aren't finished yet, my princess." He lightly squeezed her shoulders. "Dr. Kumar and I plan to investigate the entire yard to see what else, if anything, might be here."

"I appreciate what you're both doing," said Isabela, "if for nothing else, for safety's sake. And gentlemen, please send me your bill."

Dr. Wyatt smirked. "No charge as far as Devi and I are concerned. Anything to get our kids out of the house— I mean, off on another mystery!"

"Ha, ha, very funny, Dad," said Lexi. "As if we're always underfoot—*not*!"

"And we believe in neighbors helping neighbors," Dr. Kumar added with a smile.

Isabela thanked them, then suggested that she and the kids head into the house to let the men continue their work. Tomás would also arrive soon with the blueprints, and she was anxious to see her long-absent brother. The architecture firm where he interned had finally closed for vacation.

The kids followed Isabela across the lawn toward the house. Lexi was anxious to meet Tomás, but the sun was shining, and it was a beautiful day to be outside. She envied her father and Dr. Kumar getting to enjoy the warmth and birdsong. She thought it was interesting that she often wanted to be in two different places at the same time.

Isabela noticed that Lexi's thoughts had carried her far away. "Maybe some secret passages will turn up inside the house, Lexi."

Lexi nodded and smiled up at her.

"While we're waiting for Tomás, I'd like to work on the puzzle poem," Lanny said. "If we can figure out the first part, maybe we can start our search for the emerald today."

By now, the group was back inside the house. The lingering summer aromas of jasmine and privet had drifted in with them from the garden.

"Speaking of emeralds," Rani said, "did Dr. Abbott say if there was a surveillance camera in the area of the gemstone display cases? We could check that for a possible lead to the thief."

Lanny slapped his forehead. "Great idea, Rani. Why didn't I think of that?"

"Because, dear brother of mine, sometimes someone else gets to be brilliant." Lexi scrunched up her nose at him. "You gotta share the spotlight, you know."

"I'll call Dr. A right now to find out." Rani excused herself and sprinted from the room.

Isabela had just returned from getting the puzzle poem out of the wall safe and handed it to Lanny. "I'm just happy we haven't had any more strange noises or footsteps since the other night. Those unnerve me." Goosebumps rose on her arms.

"Speaking of unnerving," Moki said, "has anyone seen Madame Ronescu lately?"

"I saw her yesterday afternoon while you kids were gone, and I was in the garden," Isabela said. "Madame was apparently returning from some errands because she was carrying a large shopping bag. She took a short-cut through the cathedral churchyard. I saw her walking past the area near the crushed daisies."

"Broad daylight, Moki," Lexi said quietly with a smirk. "Convinced now she isn't a vampire?"

"But you've got to admit," he whispered, "she seems way too comfortable in graveyards for a mere mortal. Just the image of her prancing through the tombstones creeps me out. It'll probably give me a nightmare on Eucalyptus Street. Hey! That would make a great movie title."

Lexi scrunched up her lips. "Too late, Moki. It already exists—with a slight title difference—*A Nightmare on Elm Street*. Remember?"

"That's right! It stars Johnny Depp, my Mainland U.S.A. twin. What a coincidence."

Before Lexi could reply to Moki's latest digression, Rani returned with news.

"Dr. A apologized for forgetting to tell us last night about the surveillance camera. He also said the police checked, and the film was fuzzy at one point, maybe when the gems were stolen. So, either the camera wasn't working correctly, or it had been tampered with. Fortunately, no more gemstones have been stolen beyond the ten from the first theft, maybe because they posted a guard last night."

"That's good," Lanny said. "That way, we can devote most of our time today to finding the Leticia Emerald before we start looking for the exhibition's missing stones."

The others agreed.

Lanny moved to the dining room and smoothed the puzzle poem out onto the table. Everyone gathered around it. He frowned. "Can anyone make anything out of the first stanza?"

Rani read it out loud:

"Wishful dreams of bold emerald trappings
From radiant treetop and archaic wrappings;
To find what you seek, you must dash and dart
Only to discover the ending was at the start."

Everyone was silent for a moment, deep in thought.

"I think the 'wishful dreams of bold emerald trappings' means the person hunting for the stone is hopeful they will find it," Lexi said. "But I'm not sure what 'trappings' means yet."

"The next line is stranger," Rani said. "It almost sounds as if the emerald is in the treetops. But who would hide an emerald in a tree? It could fall out, get blown away, or be taken by a bird."

"And what are 'archaic wrappings'?" Moki asked.

"Maybe old, out-of-date wrappings? But what could those be? Wrapping paper, newspapers, maybe old wrapped packages or gifts?—I know! Maybe mummy bandages."

"That last idea sounds as if you're still solving our Nutmeg Street case," Lexi replied.

Rani chuckled. "Moki's got monster movies unreeling in his head."

Moki responded by making a Freddy Krueger face at them.

"Very un-handsome of you, Mr. Depp," Lexi said. She and Rani high-fived.

Lanny tuned out his friends' banter and got back to business. "The next line seems pretty obvious. We have to search hard to find the stone. But the last line is confusing. It almost sounds as if we could forget the rest of the poem because the secret to the emerald's location is in the first stanza." He scratched his head.

"But then why are there five more stanzas?" Isabela asked with a half-smile.

Lexi said, "Yeah. Good point. I'm for skipping the first stanza for now and going on to the second."

Heads nodded all around.

Moki said, "Okay, I'll read stanza two." He cleared his throat and read the lines:

"Deep down below a chamber to nourish
The players' voices, where still flourish
Wooden words helped create the magic:
Sometimes comic and sometimes tragic."

Lanny said, "It sounds like a room under the house." He snapped his fingers. "Ms. de Cordoba, do you have a cellar or a basement?"

She perked up. "Come to think of it, a large one. And as for 'nourishing players' voices,' in the cellar, there's a wooden platform my great-grandparents used as a stage where they rehearsed their parts or put on plays with their actor friends."

"You used the word 'wooden,'" Moki replied. "The line says, 'where still flourish wooden words.' How can words 'still flourish' and be 'wooden'?"

"But read the rest of it," Lexi said. Her voice raced as she took over:

"Wooden words helped create the magic:
Sometimes comic and sometimes tragic.

"That's it!" she said. "The words are their lines, probably from scripts, to create the drama, and their art still flourishes, or lives on as their legacy."

"I still don't understand why the words are 'wooden,'" Moki replied. "And what does all of that have to do with an emerald?" He scratched the back of his head vigorously.

Rani stood up. "I'm not sure, so let's head to the cellar and see if we can figure it out." Without waiting for anyone to respond, she headed out of the room.

"A great idea, Rani," Lanny said after her. He joined the march toward the kitchen.

The cellar door was accessed from the service porch. It creaked open when Isabela pulled on it. "Guess I haven't been down there in a while," she said as the group fanned away the cold, musty air racing into their nostrils. "It's unusual for California homes to have cellars, what with the ocean causing a high water table, so I don't often think about the cellar being here. But this house was built high up on Botanic Hill, so . . ."

"Ugh! Smells like rotting potatoes," Moki said. He held his nose. "Baskets and baskets of them." He let go of his nose with one hand to grip the banister to steady himself. The steep stairs were slippery from dust and mold. All at once, the group heard a cracking sound. The banister splintered under Moki's strength. He stood with a piece of it in his hands. Slowly raising his eyes, he caught Isabela gazing at him.

"Don't worry about it, Moki," she said to his surprise. "You did me a favor. This just tells me I've neglected getting this old staircase checked. It's obviously rotten with age. We de Cordobas aren't ones to change much around the house. Are you all right?"

Moki indicated he was and apologized, but Isabela stopped him. Instead, she cautioned all of them to watch for loose or decayed stairs. Fortunately, none were found.

They descended the rickety, dimly-lit steps. Rani, directly behind Isabela, brushed cobwebs aside as they went slowly down, down, down, their voices echoing slightly.

Once everyone reached the cellar floor, Isabela found another light switch and flicked it on. The cellar was enormous and in need of major cleaning. Lanny figured the area probably equaled at least half the square footage of the actual house. The group followed Isabela to an old raised platform.

"Well, here it is." She gestured toward a large stage, about fifteen feet square. Its floorboards were made from wooden slats that had various-sized gaps between them. The kids spread out and started searching it on top, around its sides, and even on its two steps. The structure creaked with age with their every move.

"Are we looking for the emerald or 'wooden words'?" Moki asked, now all business.

"Maybe both, bro," Lanny replied. He had his flashlight trained between the boards, moving methodically across every inch of the platform. "Don't forget to look between every interstice."

Moki asked, "What's an *interstice*? Immediately, his palm met his forehead with a pop. "Doh! What have I done? Delete, delete!"

Lexi groaned and said, "Well, you've done it now for sure, Moki."

She was right. Lanny the Walking Dictionary took his cue. "An interstice is a small, intervening space. In other words, a gap or space between the boards, or slats."

Moki hung his head to avoid Lexi's withering look, but Isabela said, "Good for you, Lanny, teaching new words. Why don't you other kids like it? Building a strong vocabulary is important to success in life."

Lexi said. "We don't really mind. Just not all day, *every* day as Lanny likes to do."

"Come to think of it, you're right about building word power, Ms. de Cordoba," Rani added. "Plus, I like that Lanny stays true to himself. He's smart and isn't afraid to show it." Lanny's face erupted in a smile. Lexi's did the opposite.

A few minutes later, Lanny announced, "I've found something under the stage." The interstices were wide enough in that section to give him a good look. His trusty flashlight had cast light on something square or rectangular.

Everyone froze momentarily. Were they about to find the long-lost Leticia Emerald after all these years? Then, the group circled around Lanny on a far corner of the platform.

"Is it the emerald, Lanny? Is it the emerald?" Rani asked breathlessly, waving her hands back and forth wildly.

"I don't think so," Lanny said. "It looks like a large box, way too big for an emerald, even the Leticia Emerald. Ms. de Cordoba, is it possible to break through the stage floor to get it out? I don't see any other way."

"Well, all right, if you must. Let me find a crowbar," she replied. But Moki was already walking toward the group with one he had just found. "Okay, gently," Isabela said, "though it does need repair, anyway."

She appreciated the time Moki took as he carefully

pried up as few boards as possible. Soon, Lanny and Lexi were able to lift the large, heavy box out by its side handles. Rani helped pull it up onto the stage.

It was wooden and covered with dust. Isabela found a rag and cleaned it off, reading the inscription on the top:

"May these wooden words be preserved until they are found.
All manner of joy and sorrow are herein bound."

Isabela said, "It's signed, Lorenza de Cordoba and Alondra Luna."

"Wow. May we open it?" Lanny asked with all the excitement of a true movie buff.

"Absolutely," Isabela replied. "I'm just as excited as you are to see what's inside."

They took turns trying to open the lid, not wanting to damage it by using tools other than their hands. Finally, the girls were successful, and the lid popped open with a loud squeak.

Isabela began cautiously lifting out what looked like about twenty thick manuscripts.

"Lanny, I think these are their movie scripts," Lexi said, smiling up at her brother.

"So, the 'wooden' refers to the fact that they were hidden in a wooden box?" Moki asked.

Lanny said, "Yes, or it could also mean the words are 'wooden' until brought to life by great actors." His face still beamed.

"These are my great-grandparents' scripts, all right. I recognize the titles as matching their movies. This one is for *Blue Tulips*, made in 1926. That one is for *Desert by Moonlight* from 1928. And that's for *Seaside Sonata* from 1927. Oh, this is a wonderful find."

Lanny opened one as if it were sacred. "Look. This one even has 'marginalia'—their handwritten notes and changes in the margins. That makes it even more valuable and easier to authenticate." No one objected this time over Lanny's definition.

Isabela happily skimmed through the rest. "They *all* have marginalia."

"Well, no emerald inside, but still quite a treasure from your great-grandparents," Rani said.

"Now I'm convinced the puzzle poem is a treasure hunt, and the emerald might be the grand prize," Lanny said.

Just then, the group heard a door bang shut upstairs. A voice called out in a lilt. "Hey, where is everybody? Your wonderful, handsome, intelligent brother, Tomás, is home."

"We're down here in the cellar, Tomás," Isabela shouted upward, loud enough to be heard. "Come on down and see what we've found. Watch the stairs, though. They're rickety. Better yet, come help us get these things upstairs."

A minute later, a slender, dark-haired eighteen-year-old came picking his way carefully down the stairs. He avoided the broken banister. "Isabela, what are you doing down here breathing this horrible air?" He leaped toward her and wrapped her in his arms.

"Oh, excuse me. You guys must be the detectives who've come to help find the emerald." He shook each squad member's hand. "Happy to make your acquaintances," he said. His old-world charm didn't match the slightly sweaty athletic clothes he was wearing.

"Just look what they've already found," Isabela said before the kids could reply. She plopped some of the scripts into his outstretched arms. He grunted under the weight.

Tomás studied the documents for what seemed to the others like an eternity. He barely looked at some pages, then slowed down to peruse others. It was difficult for the onlookers to await his assessment quietly.

"Wow. This is really incredible," he finally said. "Really remarkable. Voices of our relatives from the past. I'd say you've all done a great day's work. Though, not to steal any of your thunder, but now it's my turn to deliver some news. Guess what I've discovered on our house's blueprints? Get ready to be surprised twice in one day."

CHAPTER TWELVE

· ◇ ·

Going on a Lion Hunt

The group spread the scripts out on the kitchen counter. "What a haul!" Moki said. He started to wipe perspiration off his forehead but thought better of the idea once he noticed his grimy hands.

"But what should we do first?" Lexi asked. "Check out the scripts some more, or look at Tomás's blueprints?"

"I know what our movie buff Lanny wants to do," said Rani. She glanced at him, expecting he would make a grab for another script.

He surprised her. "Actually, there's a third choice. We could move on to the next puzzle poem stanza. That intruder has me worried. Time isn't on our side."

Lexi said, "Well, we have to start somewhere, so I vote for—" but Tomás cut her off.

"Excuse the interruption, Lexi, but I agree with Lanny about that intruder. The strange noises Isabela's told me about have me worried, too. Which is why I think

Isabela and I should get these valuable scripts out of the house, pronto. We can give them the attention they deserve when things are less hectic. And you kids could go on to the next stanza. Then, if you like, we can all look at the blueprints when we get back."

"Sounds like a great plan to me," said Lanny.

"Bingo! Multitasking," said Rani. She and Lanny high-fived.

Isabela asked, "But Tomás, where should we take the scripts?"

"Well, our wall safe won't hold them. That's for sure. Let's take them downtown to the bank right now before it closes and rent the biggest safe deposit box they have."

"And we four Botanic Hill Detectives will get busy on the third stanza while you're gone," said Lanny.

"And check out Tomas's blueprints when you and Ms. de Cordoba come back," said Lexi. She and Moki fist-bumped.

The plan was set. The six loaded the scripts back into the big wooden box, then into Isabela's car. She stopped right before climbing into the driver's seat and said, "Oh, Lanny, I almost forgot. You'll need me to get the poem out of the safe."

"No, thanks, Ms. de Cordoba. For right now, I think we've got something to go on already."

"What's that, bro?" Moki asked.

"Lions."

"Lions . . . lions . . . that's right, Lanny," Rani said.

She did a fist pump. "I remember the line from stanza three:

Lions' threatening stares from their moonlit perches."

Lexi cocked her head and asked, "So, Lanny, what exactly *are* we going to do?"

"While the de Cordobas are at the bank, we're going on a lion hunt all over the house and grounds to see if we can find lions on some kind of 'moonlit perches.'"

Tomás and Isabela exchanged approving nods.

She said, "Well, there certainly are a number of lions on the estate in the forms of statues, tiles, and paintings. They're the symbol of my great-grandparents' favorite movie studio, so they added them to the décor of the house. I don't have a clue about the 'moonlit perches,' though."

Tomás was also at a loss about the perches. "And I haven't even seen the puzzle poem yet, so that's something we can read when my sister and I return from the bank."

"And don't forget the blueprints and your surprise," Lexi added with a smile.

"Which reminds me. I'll go lock the blueprints in the safe right now," Tomás said. He disappeared inside but returned in no time.

The de Cordobas backed out of the driveway and were off to the bank.

✧

As the kids headed back toward the front door, Lanny turned toward his friends so abruptly that they slammed right into him.

"Hey, what's the big idea, bro?" Moki asked as he repositioned his baseball cap snuggly on his head.

"Oh, sorry, guys. Guess I'm just stressed."

Lexi rubbed her forehead's collision spot. "Ya think?"

Lanny replied, "It's just that we have to use our time wisely–and not only because of the intruder. Don't forget that we also have a case at the ARC. So, Moki, let's get busy. How about if you and I scout around outdoors? Would you girls be okay with starting on the first floor? If you have time, head to the second floor. When Moki and I finish out here, we can take the third floor."

"Yes," Rani said, then added, "and I think we should make lists of where we find lions. Maybe a few notes, too. Something that seems unimportant now may end up being very important later."

"You come up with great ideas, BFF," Lexi said, smiling once again. She squeezed Rani's arm, even though she still would have preferred to be outdoors. But exploring with Rani indoors would be fun, too.

"Wow, you guys. We've forgotten all about Dr. Wyatt and Dr. Kumar," Moki said. "They've been out in the yard since this morning. They must be doing a bang-up job. Lanny and I can check and see what they've found, if anything."

The girls agreed to the plan, then headed indoors.

"I already know where there are some lions out here," Lanny said.

"Lead the way, safari bro," Moki replied. But Lanny was already far down the sandstone path that led from the carved front door to the tall, wrought iron entry gate.

"And here we have a pair of stone lions," Lanny said. He patted one on the head. Large twin lions with blank eyes that stared, though not threateningly, did indeed flank the large gate. The boys searched every inch of the lions and the thick, square bases on which they stood but found nothing.

"Nice pair of lions, but I don't see anything that looks like moonlit perches," Moki said. "The bases aren't round like the moon." He stroked one lion's bumpy mane as if it were a pet cat.

Lanny quickly stood up straight and clasped Moki's shoulders. "Bro, you just said something brilliant."

"Me? Are you all right?" Moki covered Lanny's forehead with his hand to check for a fever.

"I'm fine," he said, pushing the boy's hand away. "You said 'round.' The 'moonlit perches' might be shapes. Maybe the shapes will be round like the moon, but not bright like moonlight."

"I don't see anything round here, so these must not be the lions we're after," Moki said. He took notes and photos with his phone. "Where to next?"

The two boys searched all around the perimeter of the

mansion. They found some clay pots in the shape of lions' heads, another smaller pair of stone lions in the flower beds, and some patio tiles with lions' faces. But nowhere could they find any round shapes that might suggest the perches. And none of the lions' eyes had "threatening stares."

"Let's go find my dad and Dr. Kumar before we go indoors," Lanny suggested.

"I'm in. Lead on, fearless safari bro." Once again, Moki had to catch up to Lanny, who was already heading around the side of the mansion.

Meanwhile, the girls were searching the first floor. Their initial find was in the entryway. Water spurted into a turquoise-and-gold-tiled alabaster basin from the mouth of a lion-head fountain, but they couldn't make out anything resembling a "moonlit perch." Rani had noticed the tiles behind the lion's head were square, so she discounted this lion's importance. Without knowing it, she had come to the same conclusion as Moki about "moonlit" meaning round moon shapes.

They found stained-glass lions in the dining room on the buffet cabinet doors, but no other lions on the first floor until they came at last to the living room.

"Rani, I never noticed these lions before," Lexi said as she pointed to two dark wooden lions' heads that flanked the fireplace. They were a magnificent pair, large and carved with ferocious scowls on their faces.

And there, to the girls' surprise, reclined Oso, watching them.

"Look at the dog, Rani. Isn't that funny? He looks as if he's waiting for us. Hi, boy. Are you trying to tell us we've found the lions?"

Oso started panting.

Rani stooped to pet him. "You know, BFF, all of us have been in this room many times, but I'm just now seeing these lions for the first time."

"If Lanny were here, he'd say that the best place to hide something is right out in plain sight," Lexi said. She joined Rani in stroking Oso. "I guess we don't always notice things until we have a reason to see them."

"Must be true. There are the 'threatening stares.'" Rani stood and traced the eyes on each with her finger. "And look. They're mounted on circular tiles. . . . Wait. Do you think? Could those circles be . . . the 'moonlit perches'?" she asked and did a small jump.

"Yes, I think you're on to something, bestie. How does the rest of that stanza go? Something about 'their eyes being turned down to the floor,' I think."

The girls spent five minutes trying to figure out how to turn the lions' eyes downward, but the eyeballs were made of solid wood and wouldn't budge. Rani made notes on her phone.

"Okay, we've covered all ten rooms downstairs, and these fireplace lions are our best bet so far," Lexi said. "But we have more to do. I'm for heading to the second floor."

"Race you," Rani said. Already heading for the staircase, she beat Lexi with little effort. Oso tagged along.

"Will I ever beat you, girlfriend? . . . Hey, it's getting dark up here."

The short-legged dog finally reached the top stair, too, huffing and puffing. The girls quickly scoured the windowless hallways, flicking on every light switch they could find as Oso watched their every move.

The three of them stayed together, searching the many guest bedrooms first. Only one contained lions. They were in a portrait of a bored-looking Egyptian queen slouching on her golden throne, her slaves fanning her with enormous ostrich plumes. Pet lions reclined on either side of her. But the girls couldn't find any round objects in the scene that would suggest the "moonlit perches." Even Oso seemed unimpressed, not engaging in any extraordinary sniffing.

"Well, that leaves Ms. de Cordoba's room," Rani said. She sighed with little nervous catches in her breath. "I remember her saying her bedroom used to belong to her great-grandparents." She turned the doorknob.

The two entered the lavender-scented bedroom to find that, unlike the hallways, there was still plenty of sunlight flooding through the numerous windows. Oso bounded in after them.

Lexi shivered. "Whoa. That's better. I'm just glad it isn't dark in here."

"You got that right, girlfriend," Rani said. "Knowing that our phantom Big Foot was in here the other night makes me anxious to finish our search and get out of here."

"Come to think of it, we haven't heard any more strange noises lately," Lexi said.

Rani rolled her eyes. "I'm all for keeping it that way. But Oso seems to want to be in here. I wonder if it's okay." The dog didn't wait for the girls to decide. He made a beeline for the fireplace.

"Looks as if it is," Lexi said. "Whatever you do, just don't let him get up on the satin bedspread." She hadn't noticed that Oso had already plopped down on the hearth.

"Hey, just curious," Lexi said. "What does the word 'noise' make you taste?"

"Snails. And their slime trails."

"Blah. Sorry I asked."

"So am I." Rani looked as if she was going to be sick, her tongue hanging from her mouth. "But let's get busy. It'll take my mind off snails."

"And their slime trails," Lexi added.

"Ugh! Enough already." Rani clutched her stomach. "Sorry I answered your question. But let's get back to business."

The girls investigated the fireplace first. The structure was made of wood painted an ivory color, but it didn't have any wooden lions. Only ornately carved angels.

They moved on to explore the far side of the room, but Oso didn't budge from the hearth. In the next instant, they heard a scraping sound behind them. The girls froze first, then turned their heads to look at each other. With eyes wide open, they slowly pivoted in the direction of the sound.

A large wooden panel on the left side of the fireplace had slid open sideways. Oso gave a low growl, then started barking ferociously. Someone—or something—was emerging from the blackness beyond. Lexi and Rani grabbed each other and let out ear-splitting screams.

CHAPTER THIRTEEN

· ◇ ·

What Sooty Walls Reveal

Startled screams aside, the girls weren't ones to shrink from a chance to capture an intruder. Just as quickly as they shrieked, they bounded toward the fireplace to tackle the figure entering the room. Oso also jumped at him, and the intruder screamed, throwing his arms up.

"What the . . . Moki!" Lexi cried out as she released her grasp. "What are you doing here? And where did you come from?"

"Just exploring your everyday secret passage with my friends here." A slightly sooty Moki grinned and pointed his thumb over his shoulder. "Hi, fella." He rubbed Oso's ear.

The girls looked behind him to find Lanny, then Dr. Wyatt, followed by Dr. Kumar.

Rani crossed her hands over her chest. "Great, but you guys nearly scared us to death. Be still, my heart."

"Sorry, but we didn't know you were here," Lanny

said. He glanced down at his clothes and brushed cobwebs off himself.

"And we didn't know where this passage led," Dr. Wyatt added.

"We ran into your dads in the garden right when they were finding this passage," Moki said.

"Wait. Wow. Woooow! A real, honest-to-goodness secret passage," Lexi said. She was now all smiles as she realized the incredible discovery.

"I was wondering how long it would take you to be happy about our find," Dad said.

"Tell us all about it," Lexi said. "Where does it start? Where does it go? How did you find it? Is this how the intruder got in and out of the house?"

"Better just to show you," Moki replied. "Follow us." He took her hand and turned to start back into the passage, but more voices in the bedroom brought him to a halt. Everyone turned to find Isabela and Tomás standing in the doorway, their mouths open in shock.

"We heard voices . . . well, what do you know?" Tomás said. He whistled as he walked toward the panel and the group. "I suspected as much from the blueprints—that was one of my surprises—but you guys have erased all doubt. This is fabulous."

Isabela introduced Tomás to the kids' fathers. Then she said, "Well, what are we waiting for? Let's explore this amazing find that's right here in our *casa*." She grabbed a flashlight from her nightstand, clicked it on, and headed toward the group. "Sorry, Oso. You stay here, and guard the rest of the house." The dog put his head down on the hearth and gave a little whine.

"We haven't had time yet to investigate the entire passage," Lanny said as he followed the others through the panel. "There appear to be at least two more branches or tunnels off this one."

Moki showed the others the small lever that, when raised or lowered, caused the panel to open or close from the inside. Then the group slowly snaked its way through the passage, crouching at points to accommodate the differing ceiling heights. They soon came to two narrow flights of stairs, one going up and one going down.

"Everything seems structurally sound and safe," Dr. Kumar said. His voice echoed in the dusty tunnel. "Going down will take us back to where we came in." He glanced at Isabela, awaiting her choice.

"Let's go down," she said. "We can explore the other passages after we look at Tomás's blueprints. I also want to see how the intruder got in and out, assuming this is how it was done."

"We think this is exactly how it was done," Lanny replied. "We aren't the first to go through here lately. We found lots of footprints inside this passageway where there should have been undisturbed dust." He beamed his flashlight toward the floor of the passage to show the others.

"Brilliant deduction, Lanny," Tomás said. "My sister

told me you were a student of Sherlock Holmes, and it shows."

Lanny turned to talk to Tomás about his favorite fictional detective but bumped his head on a beam protruding from the ceiling.

"Better watch where you're going, Mr. Holmes," Lexi said in her best whiny British accent.

"Lexi—" her father said.

"Oh, uh, sorry about that, Lanny. Sometimes, I don't think before I speak."

"That's okay, sis. Sometimes, I don't, either."

Up ahead, the group began descending a narrow wooden staircase. Then they passed through a long, earthy-smelling tunnel. Finally, Dr. Wyatt pushed hard upward on a disk-like object. Each person climbed up the rungs of a metal ladder and found themselves outside at the western edge of the de Cordoba estate. The stone wall and St. Barnabas's cathedral and churchyard were right in front of them.

They stood squinting into the late afternoon sun and surveyed the area for a minute. Then Moki said, "Your dads found the tunnel and opening. Once inside the tunnel, we found the passage."

Lexi smiled. "Way cool, Dad and Dr. Kumar. A passage—just what I wanted."

"I'd always assumed that cover was a hinged storm drain lid," Isabela said.

"Didn't your parents or grandparents know about the tunnel and passages?" Moki asked.

"If our parents knew, they never told us," Isabela said. She turned toward her brother.

Tomás said, "That's right. Plus, this tunnel isn't on the blueprints, which might mean it was added by our great-grandparents. I remember our parents saying this area of the garden used to be where the swimming pool was before the nearby piece of land was sold to the cathedral. The family moved the pool to the other side of the house to respect the cemetery's deceased and visitors."

"But since the pool was in this spot during our great-grandparents' time, maybe they put in the tunnel as a quicker way in and out of the house from here," Isabela replied.

"Ms. de Cordoba," Rani said, "the tunnel could explain how the daisies got trampled.

"Yes, Rani, since the passage opening is at the edge of the daisy patch, the intruder could have emerged here and run through the flowers to escape."

"That sounds logical," Lanny said, "but running through the flowers meant the intruder headed toward your back gardens, which took that person deeper onto your property, instead of escaping by cutting through the churchyard."

"Deeper onto the property, like to the *casita*?" Moki asked. He clutched his neck with both hands.

Lanny smirked. "Don't jump to conclusions, bro."

"The only jumping I plan to do will be to get out of Madame Countess Dracula Ronescu's way," he whispered.

"Well, I'm for investigating the rest of the passages right now," Rani said.

"Except it's getting late, and we have some other unfinished business to take care of first, remember?" Isabela asked. "Let's go indoors and look over Tomás's blueprints now. They might help us investigate the passages more efficiently."

Everyone agreed and started the long walk around the house to the patio doors. The twins' and Rani's dads had evening commitments, so they said their good-byes, even though they said they would have enjoyed exploring the remaining passages. Isabela and Tomás thanked them for unearthing the latest secrets and invited them to return anytime. The two girls lingered a bit, thanking their dads and hugging them good-bye.

The boys had already made it to the patio. Lexi and Rani quickened their steps, very anxious now to get indoors and check out Tomás's blueprints. As they entered the house, they wondered what more could be added to the mystery.

CHAPTER FOURTEEN

· ✧ ·

Blueprints and Perches

Tomás spread the blueprints out on the dining room table. The kids and Isabela gathered around him. "See? No underground tunnel here," he said as he pointed to the daisy patch area.

"Then it had to have been built by our great-grandparents," Isabela replied.

Lexi tried to understand the blueprints. "Where are the other secret passages on here?"

"See what look like double walls, here and here?" Tomás said, pointing to specific areas. "Those are what I guessed to be possible passages. Now we know for sure some of them are."

"It looks as if there are passages going to all the floors, including the attic," Rani said. "That would explain the purpose of the other narrow staircases that we saw in the passage."

Lexi snapped her fingers. "Hey, I almost forgot. Rani

and I think we found the 'lions with threatening stares on moonlit perches.' They're on the fireplace in the living room! The blueprints show double walls there. Let's go see if we can find an opening."

"Whoohoo!" shouted Moki. He galloped into the living room with the others right behind him.

Tomás brought the blueprints. Isabela stopped to remove the puzzle poem from the safe in case they needed it and handed it to Lanny.

Lanny took the poem and thanked her. "Let's review what stanza three says."

Tomás looked over Lanny's shoulder at the writing, seeing it now for the first time. Lanny read out loud:

"Lions' threatening stares from their moonlit perches
Warn of danger for would-be explorers' searches.
But once their eyes are turned down to the floor,
The way becomes clear, it reveals much more."

Rani pointed to the carved lions and their eyes. "See? There are the lions with their 'threatening stares.' They are warning us, the 'would-be explorers,' to frighten us away."

"And the round disks they're mounted on might be the 'moonlit perches,'" Lexi said.

"Moki thought the same thing about the shapes being round like the moon," Lanny said. He slapped his friend on the back.

Moki's attention, however, remained fixed on the lions. "But we have a big problem, guys. How can their eyes be 'turned down to the floor'?"

Rani snapped her fingers. "Hey, I know. We need to look for some kind of lever or button near them that might turn their eyes downward."

"Brilliant, Rani," Lanny said.

Moki and Lanny explored one lion, and the girls took the other. Isabela and Tomás looked on in amazement at how clever these kids were at problem solving.

Soon, Moki said, "I think I've found something. There's a little button in this lion's mane." He pushed it. Instantly, there was a slight clicking sound, and the lions' wooden heads slowly turned downward, their eyes now staring at the hearth. A few seconds later, the group heard rumbling, and a tall, narrow panel to the left of the fireplace slid open sideways, just as the one in Isabela's room upstairs had done.

"You're a genius, Moki," Lexi said. She hugged him, and he made no attempt to stop her.

"Well, the lions might be looking down, but things are looking up for me," Moki replied. "First, Lanny says I'm brilliant about the round shapes. Now you call me a genius and give hugs. This is my lucky day."

"This is all our lucky day," Rani said. "Come on." She waved the group forward and, once again, they entered a hidden passage. It was also dusty, and the grime had been disturbed like in the passage they had already explored.

"Wow. Look at all the footprints. And what's this?" Lanny asked. He bent down and picked up a rectangular, metal object and soon recognized it as an old portable cassette recorder. "Hmm, I'll bet the intruder's been recording what's been said in the living room, but we can't know for sure since the cassette is missing." The others gathered around to inspect the device.

"Well, that's possible according to the blueprints. The living room is right on the other side of this wall," Tomás said. Lanny scrunched up his nose.

Isabela raised her hand to her mouth in shock. "Then the person might have heard me read the puzzle poem that first night when we also heard the footsteps upstairs."

"And might have recorded the poem to use it to find the emerald before we do," Lanny replied. "I'll bring this machine with us so it can't be used again."

"Yikes," Lexi said, looking at Rani. "We might be having a race now, not just a hunt."

Moki said, "If the intruder stayed in a passage for a while, that could explain why we didn't see any wet, muddy footprints that rainy night."

"Well, here's something the intruder didn't find," Tomás said. He had gone ahead of the group and found a small lever covered by cobwebs on a wall. Everyone joined him to inspect it. "Unless I miss my guess . . ."

He dusted it off and tried pushing it upward. The lever slowly yielded under his strength.

With a loud screech, a part of the wall facing them slowly slid sideways.

CHAPTER FIFTEEN

· ✧ ·

The Secret Room

With his hand extended, Tomás said, "I present to you a secret room." The group bent forward and peered inside the musty space revealed by the sliding wall. "I suspected its existence after studying the blueprints."

Isabela slowly stepped inside. "What could have been the purpose of this room?"

"Some people used to build what was called a *safe room* into their homes," Tomás explained. "If someone broke into the house, the family could hide in the room undetected. Maybe that's what this is."

"Well, it looks as if it had an additional purpose," Lanny said. He held up a large sword still in its elaborately decorated scabbard. A dingy white-fringed tassel hung from the hilt's guard.

"Look at these," Rani said. She picked up a tarnished silver hairbrush and a blackened hand mirror.

Moki carefully unrolled a huge fragile piece of paper

that showed Lorenzo and Alondra starring in *Royal Rhapsody,* one of their classic films from 1925. "You don't have to be Lanny to know this is a movie poster."

Lexi reported from a far corner, "And check this out. A tiny desk with a chair and an embroidered seat cushion. How pretty." Her flashlight revealed their beauty.

"I'd say we've found more of your great-grand-parents' treasures," Lanny said. "I believe these are props and marquee sheets from some of their silent movies."

Isabela and Tomás beamed over yet another discovery.

The group soon forgot time while examining the furniture and souvenirs of the family's movie trade. After what must have been at least an hour, the kids wandered out into the passage to continue exploring.

Isabela said, "Not now, guys. I hate to be a killjoy, but remember? The intruder has been in this passage. We need to take these props and things upstairs to Tomás's room for safekeeping tonight. There don't seem to be any secret passages leading into his room—as far as I could tell from the blueprints."

"I think you're right, sis. Wish I'd realized that earlier. It might have saved us a trip to the bank to rent that safe deposit box."

"I'm not sorry we went," Isabela replied. "I know for certain those scripts will be safe. And like those, I'm sure these items are old and historically valuable. Well, it looks as if we'll have a late dinner tonight, I'm afraid."

Moki stifled a groan.

The group made its way back to the passage entrance. Oso had been faithfully waiting for them there in the living room. He followed his owners and the detectives up and down the house stairs with each trip they made to secure the newly discovered treasures in Tomás's room on the second floor.

"You stay out of those passages, Oso, or we might never find you," Isabela said. She shook her finger at her dog, then smiled and patted him on his cocked head.

"So, Rani," Tomás said from nearby as he carried two ornate silver candelabra upstairs, "my sister tells me you have synesthesia. What does my name make you taste?"

"Spaghetti sauce," she replied instantly while jostling a heavy box of movie posters.

"And how about Madame Ronescu?" Moki asked, eavesdropping.

"You asked me that before. The taste hasn't changed, and you still don't want to know." Rani puckered up her face.

"There's something not right about that woman," Moki said to Lexi. "Rani proves it."

"Moki, Rani's synesthesia doesn't necessarily mean that Madame R is a suspect."

"But don't you remember in our last case on Nutmeg Street, we discovered that two people were actually one and the same person, and Rani had tasted mac 'n' cheese both times?"

"Thanks, Moki," Rani said, "but there's still no proof my synesthesia can help us solve any mysteries . . . though, my ability did *seem* to help us as you said. Well, probably just a coincidence."

"Moki, just think what Lanny would say if he had heard you," Lexi said. "He'd say, 'It's all about evidence, evidence, and more evidence.'"

"Maybe it's because I'm hungry," Moki said. "I can smell Ms. Tina's salsa and chicken enchiladas calling to me from the kitchen." He hung his head for dramatic effect.

Once the secret space was emptied, and all its treasures were stowed in Tomás's room, Lanny said, "Well, still no emerald. Again, this new discovery seems to show that we are definitely on a treasure hunt all over the estate. But we've done a lot of work today, and dinner will be ready soon. I suspect Ms. de Cordoba will want us to wait until tomorrow morning to tackle the fourth stanza and to continue to explore the passages."

"Well, if we have to wait . . ." Lexi said.

But Lanny hadn't really convinced himself about delaying, not even for dinner.

"And we should call Dr. Abbott to see if any more jewels went missing," Moki said.

Lanny sighed deeply. "You're right, bro. Our other case." His mouth puckered, and his brows pinched together.

"I think there's at least one more thing we must do—and *tonight*," Rani said. "Close off the passages in the living room and in Ms. de Cordoba's room to keep the intruder out."

"An excellent suggestion, Rani," Isabela said. "How

about using some wooden pegs that we can jam between the panels and the walls? That way, the intruder won't be able to slide open the panels."

Tomás took his cue and went to the garage workshop to look for something to use.

He returned shortly with some pegs that would work perfectly. "Of course, we know there are more passages, so there could be more sliding panels, too," he said. "Everyone, be on guard. Buddy up, lock your doors, and listen for any noises."

Once the pegs were in place and Tomás's bedroom door lock checked, the group headed to the dining room for a Mexican feast. But it wasn't hunger pains gnawing at Lanny. It was the delay. Before the group reached the dining room, he stopped dead in his tracks. The others did the same—without bumping into him for a change. Lanny turned toward Isabela.

"Ms. de Cordoba, I hope you won't think I'm rude if I ask you if you can get the puzzle poem for me out of the safe right now—before dinner.

"Not at all, Lanny. You're certainly a dedicated detective."

"Actually, I'm really convinced we're now in a race against the intruder for the emerald. Maybe for more of your family treasures, too. The footprints in the passages, the tape recorder, and the noises we've heard have made me nervous. They're telling me that time is not on our side. We have to hurry."

Isabela said, "All right, Lanny, come with me. Everyone else, please be seated for dinner. We'll join you in a minute."

While the two detoured to the safe, everyone else filed into the dining room with Moki in the lead. He pulled out his chair so quickly it banged against the table leg, causing some clattering of the silver, crystal, and china place settings. He was glad Ms. de Cordoba hadn't witnessed his carelessness.

Within a moment, Lanny and Isabela joined the others, and the group dived into the feast. Lanny's appetite didn't match the amount of food he heaped onto his plate. He knew he was distracted by the poem next to him on the table, but he didn't want to offend Isabela by not eating. After one bite of food, however, he set his fork down.

With Isabela's permission, he recited the lines for the group:

"An artisan's tilework leads to loftier places
Where there are myriad quarters with timeworn traces.
When the sunlight's ray strikes the portrait at three,
Look to the jeweled hand that recommends your knee.

"Any thoughts?" Lanny asked.

"Yeah, I think I'll have another enchilada," Moki said as he looked for the large platter. Tomás passed it to him.

Lexi glared at Moki. "Duh. He means about the poem."

"To prove that I was listening," Moki said, "I think the 'artisan's tilework leading to loftier places' refers to the ginormous staircase in the entryway. It has colorful tilework on each step, and it goes to 'loftier places,' namely, the floors upstairs."

"You do surprise me sometimes," Lexi said. "Here, have some more chips and guacamole." Moki gladly obliged.

"What could 'myriad quarters with timeworn traces' mean?" Isabela asked.

Rani swallowed a forkful of refried beans before speaking. "Well, 'myriad' means many. 'Quarters' could be coins, but I think in this case 'quarters' are rooms— many timeworn rooms," Rani said slowly, then brightened and snapped her fingers. "That's it. So maybe we're supposed to look in the rooms your great-grandparents had assumed would become timeworn by your family's presence for some reason."

Isabela dabbed her mouth with her napkin. "That has to refer to the third-floor rooms the family has never fully used, not even since the house was built. Probably the 'myriad' guest bedrooms, offices, and sitting rooms up there. Places that might get shabbier over time from neglect."

"Whoa, whoa, whoa," said Moki. He positioned his hands in a time-out signal. "Back up, please. I don't understand. It sounds as if your great-grandfather assumed things wouldn't be moved around much over the years. No portraits removed from the walls, or fireplaces remodeled after all these years? The same rooms unused? Sounds unbelievable."

Lanny enjoyed witnessing Moki's occasional perceptivity, which he sensed Moki often hid so his friend could appear to be the brainy one. It was even more fun to see Moki in a rare moment when an idea made him forget about the food right in front of himself.

Tomás understood Moki's confusion. "Let me explain, Moki. In large ancestral homes like this, few things are ever changed. No one in the de Cordoba family has wanted to destroy what is referred to as the historical integrity of the house. It's our family's tradition to keep things the same as much as possible for each succeeding generation."

"That sounds more like a European concept than an American one," Rani said.

"You might be right," Tomás said. "Our roots are European. It is a de Cordoba tradition to preserve our family's past, and that tradition has been handed down generation to generation—from our great-great-grandfather Emilio, to great-grandfather Lorenzo, then to our grandfather Valentino, and to our father Diego."

"But objects probably have to be removed for cleaning or restoring," Moki said.

"Yes, but later, the objects in this house are always put back right where they were," Tomás replied. "There has been restoration work done here but little remodeling. If any changes are ever made, they are supposed to be recorded in our family's repair journal."

Lexi drained her glass of milk and said, "I can think of an American example where repairs and furnishing are documented—the White House. The White House Historical Society in Washington, D.C., catalogues those kinds of things, especially if a new presidential family wants to change anything."

Isabela replied, "That's right, Lexi. And the only entries in our *La Casa de los Árboles* estate repair journal have to do with plumbing and electrical repairs or upgrades, the swimming pool move, some exterior stucco work, a new roof, a few additional pieces of furniture, and some major landscaping. As to the art in the house, it's valuable for financial and sentimental reasons, so it hasn't been moved. If it had been, it would have been catalogued. I feel confident in saying my great-grandparents probably assumed nothing would upset the chain of clues in the poem—if they even considered that at all, given the family tradition of uniformity."

Lanny looked up from his plate, still full of food. "Was there any mention of the secret tunnel from the old swimming pool to the house?"

"Hmm. Strange, but I don't remember one," Isabela replied. "That is a break from tradition." She looked to her brother to see if he had any ideas about it.

"My guess is our great-grandparents just wanted to keep it a secret among themselves and their Hollywood friends. Our grandparents and parents didn't seem to know about it." Tomás added, "And the passages—they had to have been built at the same time as the house and were on the blueprints, so there would be no reason to list those in the house journal."

Isabela added, "As to the third floor, we actually do use it more now than our ancestors did, but the artwork, other than for cleaning, and the rooms' architectural features definitely haven't been disturbed."

"Yeah, I have to admit that sometimes I get tired of these preservation traditions," Tomás said to the kids. "One time, I suggested to my sister that we turn one of the rooms up there into a card room and have poker-and-pizza nights." Isabela shot him a friendly stink eye over the table's flower centerpiece.

Tomás laughed and said, "I didn't suggest *that* again."

The kids laughed with him.

Moki whistled. "Well, poker room or no poker room, it's lucky for all of us and the emerald hunt that the traditions continued, or we'd be up a creek without a surfboard." Not forgetting he was at the dinner table, he spooned up some dessert that Tina had just set in front of him.

Lanny declined the dish of flan but thanked Tina, anyway. "Getting back to the poem, I think we can narrow down which room by using the next two lines in the stanza. We're looking for the room with a portrait of someone with a 'jeweled hand.' That might mean a ring on a finger or a bracelet on a wrist."

"And the 'sunlight's ray striking the portrait at three' could refer to time," Lexi said.

EUCALYPTUS STREET: GREEN CURSE

"Yeah, we have to find the portrait with a jeweled hand that has sunlight striking it at three o'clock," Moki said. "May I please have some more dessert?"

Tina set Lanny's helping in front of Moki.

"But 'the hand recommending your knee' has me confused," Rani said.

"Well, maybe that part will become clear once we find the portrait," Lanny replied.

Since Lanny had eaten very little of his dinner, Moki reached over to spear his friend's enchilada with his fork. Instead, Isabela quickly pointed to the nearby platter from which he could help himself.

Lanny said, "And there's one more piece that can help narrow our search. If the sun 'strikes the portrait at three,' then we're looking for portraits facing west and across from windows where the sun would enter the house in the middle of the afternoon."

"Lanny, that's brilliant," Isabela said.

"Very Sherlock Holmes of you," added Tomás. The boy's blush almost matched the bright red salsa that had pooled on his plate.

Within a matter of minutes, a more relaxed Lanny gave a big yawn. It was contagious. Even Moki yawned between bites of his flan. Everyone agreed it had been an amazing and productive day.

Not long after dinner, the documents were locked in the safe, and the group headed to bed to await the next day's adventures.

As they trudged up the stairs, Tomás elbowed Moki and whispered, "Don't let my sister fool ya. She's a great poker player." He winked, and the group said goodnight.

CHAPTER SIXTEEN

· ✧ ·

Exploring in the Dark

Everyone slept soundly after all their exertion hauling the secret room treasures upstairs, then deciphering another portion of the puzzle poem.

Hours later, however, Lanny was awakened by four gongs from the grandfather clock in the first-floor entryway. He lay there listening to Moki's occasional tossing and turning and was about to drift back to sleep. But a new sound reached his ears. Soft footsteps were coming from the room directly overhead. Someone was on the third floor!

"Moki, wake up," he whispered to his friend in the other twin bed.

Moki didn't budge.

Lanny went over and shook him vigorously.

"Huh, what'sup, bro?" Moki said too loudly.

"Shhh. You and I are heading to the room above ours. I just heard something up there."

"Why don't you go, then come back and tell me what you found," his groggy friend replied. "Besides, our parents told us we're not supposed to go creeping around, remember?" He pulled the covers back over his head, but Lanny yanked them off.

"Our parents told us it's okay to explore as long as we stick together, remember? And we agreed to spend nights here until the emerald was found. So, come on. I'm stronger than you think, dude. Don't make me drag you out of bed. We just might catch the intruder."

"Now you're talking my language," Moki said. "Well, not actually Hawaiian, but I get it."

The boys stepped out into the dark, empty hallway. Apparently, no one else had heard the sound. Lanny didn't want to risk waking the others by turning on the hall lights, so he flicked on his flashlight instead. Moki did the same. The beams cast elongated shadows upward toward the high ceiling. The two boys moved silently and quickly on tiptoes toward the spiral staircase at the end of the long hall. After climbing it, thankfully managing to avoid the creaky stairs, they found that they had reached an equally dark corridor on the third floor. Lanny didn't know where the hall light switch was, but he wanted to keep the area as dark as possible, anyway. No need to announce their approach.

Their eyes had adjusted to the darkness. Lanny pointed to the door of the suspected room and flashed Moki an A-OK sign. They turned off their flashlights, noticing the room's door was slightly ajar, and listened for any sounds. Nothing but the mournful "who-who" sound of the resident barn owl in the old magnolia tree outside. They waited two more minutes, shivering and wishing they hadn't forgotten their bathrobes and slippers. Still no sounds came from the room. Even the owl became silent. Moki felt the hair on the back of his neck stand up.

Finally, Lanny pushed the door open slightly and slipped into the room. Moki followed. Their flashlights stayed off to give them the element of surprise and to prevent spooking a possible intruder. Finally, after what seemed like an hour, not minutes, and still hearing nothing, Lanny flicked on his flashlight. He trained the light around the space, focusing first on the walls and furniture to see if there were any secret panels opened or items disturbed. Nothing seemed out of the ordinary.

Nothing, that is, until Moki yelled, "Something just hit my leg!" He tried to turn on his flashlight but was too unnerved by the occurrence.

Lanny quickly shone his flashlight toward Moki's feet and saw a flurry of activity.

Lanny exhaled. "Hey, bro, look down at what scared you."

Moki obeyed. To his great relief, there was Oso, looking up at the boys. He panted and wagged his tail. Lanny found the wall switch and turned on the ceiling light.

"Oh, man. What's the dog doing up here?" Moki asked. He was slightly embarrassed but secretly relieved they hadn't come face to face with a real intruder. He was also glad his yell apparently hadn't awakened anyone downstairs. Bending down, he stroked the dog's head. "Aloha, Oso."

Lanny said, "Maybe he sleeps here. But I'll tell you what I really think. I think Oso heard something just as I did. And like us, he came up here to investigate, didn't you, old buddy?" Lanny bent down and ruffled the dog's ears.

"Let's see what happens if I let go of his collar," Lanny said. As he suspected, Oso resumed sniffing around the room. He gave special attention to the walls.

"Look at him go. I think you're right about that, bro," Moki said. "Hey, could this be the room with the portrait with the jeweled hand that was mentioned in the puzzle poem?"

"Good idea, but it can't be. This room faces east, not west. Remember? We're looking for a room where the mid-afternoon sunlight strikes the portrait."

Lanny glanced around but found no works of art. The room looked like an antiquated office with an ancient typewriter, framed photos, and a dusty cubby for sorting papers on top of a heavy, carved mahogany desk.

Lanny whispered, "Moki, I'm convinced the intruder is trying to solve the poem step by step with us because of the tape recorder we found in the secret passage. If that intruder has also figured out our current poem stanza, they have to be looking for the portrait like us . . . and maybe on this floor like us."

"Well, I say we can investigate this room better by daylight."

"Right, Moki. And we should. Maybe there's a secret passage in here. The blueprints might show us later this morning."

Soon, Oso grew bored and plodded back downstairs. The boys decided to do a quick check of the remaining rooms on the floor to rule out a hidden intruder. Moki flipped off the overhead light as they exited the office. Again they tiptoed in the hall.

Moki opened the next door and gasped, almost dropping his flashlight. The beam revealed ghostly forms! But they were just sheet-draped furniture. Now, the boys knew to expect such scenes, so they weren't surprised by them anymore as they inspected the remaining seven rooms. They heard no more noises and saw no intruders.

The two detectives descended the cold, spiral staircase as noiselessly as they had climbed it thirty minutes before. They gladly tumbled into their beds and pulled the thick covers over their heads.

Soon, they fell soundly asleep despite the owl resuming its plaintive night call outside.

CHAPTER SEVENTEEN

· ✧ ·

Handy Work Above

"**I** like what you eat around here," Moki said to Isabela at the breakfast table the next morning. He yawned and debated between more sleep or food. Food won out. "Huevos rancheros, and it's only Thursday. That's what my dad and I have on weekends. Have you ever had them with a side of pineapple? Delicious and nutritious."

"You'll have to make do with mixed fruit today," Isabela said. She mustered a half-smile as she passed him the bowl.

"Works for me—uh, I mean, thanks," Moki replied. He accepted the crystal bowl brimming with a rainbow of fresh fruit and pursed his lips. *Note to self, note to self, think before you speak!* he said inside his head.

Lanny updated the group on the footsteps and his and Moki's investigation earlier that morning on the third floor. Oso's sleuthing was included in the retelling, especially his sniffing the walls. "Ms. de Cordoba, could we have a good look at the blueprints this morning? They might help us figure out where the passages and panels are before we actually explore any more of them or the upstairs rooms."

"That sounds like an excellent idea," Isabela said. She excused herself, set her napkin by her plate, and rose to get them from the safe.

Rani popped a strawberry into her mouth. "And don't forget we have to find the portrait with the 'jeweled hand' by three o'clock this afternoon, so we can see the sunlight striking it."

"I'm sorry I'm not more familiar with the portraits on the third floor," Tomás said, "but there are just so many of them. Isabela and I have never really studied the mansion's artwork in depth. As much as we respect and preserve the art legacy of the family for its sentimental value, we just aren't 'art people.'"

"I think checking the secret passages is as important as finding the portrait," Lanny said. "Those footsteps I heard made me suspect the intruder may be ahead of us in the search for the emerald."

Isabela rejoined the group and handed Lanny the blueprints before sitting back down.

Lexi spooned up more fruit. "Well, we know there are more passages because we saw some when we explored the first time and when we found the secret room."

"How about if we split up?" Moki suggested. "Tomás, Lanny, and I can use the blueprints and explore the passages, and Ms. de Cordoba, Lexi, and Rani, can look for the portrait upstairs." After what happened with the breakfast fruit, Moki thought it best to put some distance between himself and Isabela. Plus, he liked Tomás's easygoing, less formal nature.

Isabela said, "Great idea, Moki. And maybe we'll all meet up in the process."

Just then, Lexi's phone vibrated in her pocket. Her eyes grew big. "Oh, oh! It's Dr. Abbott. I hope it's not bad news." She asked to be excused and took the call in the kitchen.

The others continued discussing the need to look for the portrait in rooms facing west. When Lexi returned, she said, "Listen to this. Mr. Abercrombie, the ARC's guard on duty near the gemstones exhibit, was knocked unconscious sometime last night." Everyone in the room gasped. "Fortunately, he's okay now. But this morning, Dr. A and Mr. Dayton discovered ten more gemstones missing. This time, the thief took the ones that are the most valuable in today's market."

Rani's fork clattered to her plate. "Oh, sorry about that, Ms. de Cordoba. You mean the really valuable emeralds, rubies, and diamonds?"

"That's right," Lexi replied. "All priceless, according to Dr. A."

Moki stopped eating. "What did the police say? Was my dad there to help?"

"Your dad was there. He and the other officers looked at the surveillance tape, and just like the first instance, they saw static during the time they think the theft occurred."

"The thief must know electronics and have a way into the building," Moki said.

"That's what everyone's thinking," Lexi replied. "The alarm wasn't triggered, either."

"Maybe the thief had keys," Lanny said.

"For the doors and the display cases, too?" Rani asked. "Seems a stretch. How would they get them?"

"Well, there weren't any signs of forced entry," Lexi said. "And remember how Mr. Dayton told us he had briefly lost his keys in the city before he came here? I told Dr. A we'd come by as soon as possible, but it might not be until tomorrow." She returned her phone to vibrate and put it back into her pocket.

"Good point about the keys, Lexi," Lanny said. "Yeah, with the work we have to do here, I doubt we can get there until tomorrow. All the more reason for us to get busy here and now."

The kids helped carry the breakfast dishes into the kitchen. Tina said she'd do the cleanup, which freed the others to study the blueprints. Tomás spread them out on a nearby table.

"As I figure it, there are four passages and the tunnel," he said. "The first passage was from the living room that led to the safe room. From there, I remember we saw two staircases. We already explored the one that descends to connect to the tunnel that goes outside. We know about the second passage going up to Isabela's room." Tomás traced each passage on the blueprints and where the stairs were as he remembered them. No one could take their eyes off the detailed pages.

Isabela pointed to the wide spaces between the walls. "A third passage, here, seems to go to the third floor, probably by way of more stairs from the passage going to my room."

Rani jabbed at the image of a room with the passage behind it and said, "That must be the room Lanny, Moki, and Oso—the *fifth* Botanic Hill Detective—investigated last night."

"I think you're right, Rani—at least about the room. Not sure yet about Oso's abilities!" Tomás said with a smile.

Moki pointed to the passage. "I remember seeing a set of stairs going up near there."

"Yes. I chose for us to go down yesterday, so the area going up needs to be explored," Isabela said.

Lanny said, "If the intruder was in the house last night, the person must have used that very passage and the stairs to get to the third floor. Let's hope the intruder hasn't solved the puzzle poem."

"Maybe they weren't interested in the third floor but were actually going to the attic," Lexi said. She pointed to the fourth passage leading there. "We seem to be finding everything but the emerald so far, so maybe there are more hidden treasures from the old Hollywood days."

"I hope so," Lanny said. His love of the classic

movies momentarily overrode his desire to find the emerald ahead of the intruder.

The entire group liked Moki's plan for the day's exploration. The girls and Isabela were going to focus on finding the portrait in third-floor rooms facing west. The boys and Tomás decided to limit their search to the stairs and passages pertaining to the third floor. If time permitted, and Lanny hoped it would, they would head to the highest passage leading to the attic.

Lexi said, "I still remember the lines from the puzzle poem:

When the sunlight's ray strikes the portrait at three,
Look to the jeweled hand that recommends your knee."

"Well, it's a sunny day," Rani said. "That should help. And maybe we'll find out what 'your knee' has to do with anything."

The guys took high-power flashlights to use in the passages, opting not to use their phones' lights. Tomás found a lantern. Next, the group moved to the living room. The girls and Isabela watched as Moki pushed the button that turned the lions' eyes down. The guys disappeared through the sliding panel in the fireplace and closed the door behind themselves, just in case Detective Oso got curious and wanted to follow.

The dog was actually outside on the patio where he loved to sunbathe every morning. Fortunately, the weather in Las Palmitas accommodated this habit most days. Isabela was glad he was occupied and that the panel closed. She didn't want her pet getting lost in the passages. Then, the girls and Isabela headed for the third floor, using the house stairs.

After reaching their destination, Isabela flicked on the hall lights. "This side of the hallway has rooms facing west. There are six rooms down this side. All their windows face west where the sun can enter, so there should be plenty of light. But turn on whatever ceiling lights you need."

"How about if we each take two of the rooms?" Lexi asked. "That way, we should find the portrait in no time."

"Yes, BFF, and whoever thinks she's found the portrait can call out to the others," Rani said.

Isabela agreed to the plan and chose the two adjacent rooms closest to her. Lexi took the middle two rooms, leaving Rani with the two at the end of the hallway. They wished each other good luck and set off.

The rooms Isabela searched consisted of her late grandparents' bedroom and its sitting room. She could still smell Grandmother Ana Sophia's spicy, pungent perfume that lingered in the fabric. Isabela's father, Diego, had told her stories about how her grandfather, Valentino, had brought the perfume back for his wife from Spain. Happier childhood times flooded upon her. She shook her head mildly to force herself to stick to the important task at hand.

Though Isabela had seen the rooms draped in sheets

often enough before, they looked off-putting to her now under the circumstances. She peeked behind the coverings to look at the paintings. They were all pastorals, or country scenes, showing farmers and shepherds from bygone days in old Mexico.

Lexi's search took her to two large guest bedrooms. One had burgundy and dark green décor. The other was painted shades of pink. Like the previous rooms, their furnishings were draped, and it took time to push the heavy sheets aside to make a thorough search. In the pink room, she found a tall, leaded glass display cabinet with beautiful multicolored miniature vases. In all, the two rooms had ten portraits, she assumed of de Cordoba ancestors—but no hands with jewelry.

Meanwhile, the boys and Tomás traveled through the narrow passages from the living room fireplace to the one just adjacent to Isabela's room. "Here are the stairs to the third floor," Moki said. He pointed to them with his flashlight until Tomás's lantern could illuminate them fully to the group. They noticed fresh footprints on the dusty stairs, reinforcing the urgency of their search.

"Just like the passages, the stairs are dark and narrow," Lanny said. "Apparently, the builders had to make everything fit within a three-foot-wide space."

"And they wanted to create passages that weren't obvious from outside the walls," Tomás added.

Moki said, "I'd say they succeeded, considering you've lived here all your life and didn't know about these secret spaces until now."

He squeezed his muscular frame up the stairs and was already half-way up to the third-floor passage. Once he arrived, Moki said, "Check this out. More footprints up here, too. Must be from the person Lanny heard last night."

There was no doubt someone else had gotten to the area ahead of them.

Deep frown lines crossed Lanny's forehead. "One more passage and another set of stairs after this to the attic if we have time. And I repeat, I hope we do." His voice had a worried tone not lost on Moki who followed behind him.

"I wonder how the girls' and Ms. de Cordoba's searches are going," Moki said.

Tomás was behind them. "Speaking of searches, we can't forget to keep searching the walls carefully for hidden levers."

Back on the third floor, Rani had almost completed her search of the office and guest bedroom. Still no calls from the other two, so she was about to give up hope of any of them having good luck. But luck changed. When she pushed aside the last sheet-draped work of art, she saw what they had been looking for. It was a portrait of a young cavalier with long, dark hair and a plumed hat. She thought he looked somewhat like Tomás. The sword in his right hand was raised, but the left hand was near his side with the index finger seeming to point diagonally across the painting to its outer edge. There, on his left index finger, was a gold-filigree band containing an enormous painted ruby.

Rani hadn't turned on the lights or opened the draperies, so she clicked on her flashlight instead. When the beam hit the red stone, it shimmered intensely against the glittery paint. Her brown eyes lit up like the ring.

"Hey, Lexi, Ms. de Cordoba," she yelled. "Come see what I've found."

The two soon appeared next to Rani and gazed at the portrait's sparkling stone.

"Wow. Hey, bestie, I think you found it!" shouted Lexi. She hugged her friend.

Isabela beamed. "I agree. Good work, Rani. Congratulations!"

Isabela moved across the room and pushed open the heavy red velvet drapes that covered the floor-to-ceiling window. Dust particles danced in the intense light. The room was instantly flooded with sunshine, and a view of the house's west side yard was revealed.

Lexi sighed. "Darn. It's only one o'clock. Guess we'll have to wait two more hours to see the sun's ray strike the portrait." Her shoulders sagged.

Before anyone could respond, the girls and Isabela were startled to hear a scuffling sound coming from behind the ruby-ring portrait. With quizzical expressions, they stared straight ahead. Within seconds, the seven-foot-tall work of art slowly swung silently outward like a hinged door.

"Whoa," Lexi said, pushing the others back. The three almost knocked each other down trying to get out of the way. Behind the painting was a staircase with five ascending steps. A figure noisily descended them. His face became visible as he ducked his head to enter the room.

"Aww, Moki again!" said Lexi. "You almost gave us another heart attack."

Rani and Isabela let out sighs of relief. Moki laughed, then apologized for scaring them.

A few seconds later, Lexi said, "Wow. This is one awesome panel entrance."

Moki smiled mischievously. "It's all in the flick of a lever." His flashlight beam pointed out the switch's location at the top of the short staircase. "You know, Ms. de Cordoba, you've got one cool house here."

She smiled and thanked him as Lanny and Tomás clomped down the steps.

"Wow. But look what you three have found," Lanny said. "The portrait with the jeweled hand."

"That's the good news," Lexi replied. "I was just saying that the bad news is we still have two more hours until three o'clock."

"I have an idea," Rani said. "Let's simulate three o'clock. Maybe if we all shine our flashlights on the portrait, the hand might just show us how it 'recommends your knee.'"

Moki flicked on his flashlight. "Good thinking, but where on the portrait?"

"Let's try concentrating our light on the ring," Rani said, "since, according to the puzzle poem, the hand is doing the recommending." She turned to look behind her out the window to get a bearing, then back again at the portrait. "Plus, I think the sunlight *would* most likely strike the hand at three o'clock."

Everyone thought these were ingenious ideas, especially since Lanny felt time was favoring the intruder. Five flashlights and a lantern were immediately aimed at the ring.

Instantly, a huge prism of light emanated from the glittery material contained within the ring's paint. A rainbow was cast across the wall to the right, puddling on the floor.

"That's it," Lanny said. He quickly dropped to his knees. "Hey, our knees! We have to kneel on the floor. That's what it meant." He glanced down. "There must be something hidden under these floorboards where the light spectrum is pointing."

"OMG. Maybe it's finally the emerald," Rani said.

Lexi grasped her friend's arm, squeezing a bit too hard as was her bad habit. Rani gently removed her bestie's hands.

"A treasure at the end of the rainbow," Lexi said. The two hugged each other.

It felt like forever to the kids as they waited for

Sherrill Joseph

Tomás to fetch some tools to pry up the floorboards. By the time he returned—only a few minutes later—it was everything they could do just to contain their excitement. Isabela grabbed a hammer and used the claw end to begin the task carefully so as to minimize the damage to the floor.

"Just pound right into the wood, Ms. de Cordoba," Moki said, but his pleading landed on deaf ears. Care won out this time.

"No way, Moki. This house was a precious gift handed down by generations of my family, and for future generations. I won't destroy one treasure in a hunt for another."

Moki resorted to silently pacing the room in his excitement.

One by one, Isabela and Tomás removed three short floorboard segments. Finally, the hole was big enough for a good look. Lanny trained his flashlight inside. Everyone craned their necks to see.

Inside was a metal box about one-foot-square. It was covered with decades of dust.

Rani lifted it out and—with surprising effortlessness—popped open the lid.

CHAPTER EIGHTEEN

· ✧ ·

Up the Attic Stairs

Moki stared inside the box along with everyone else. "Just pictures? A box of pictures?"

"No. Not 'just pictures,' bro. Photos. Movie stills. Over one hundred of them, I'd say," Lanny replied with a huge smile. "Wow. This is phenomenal."

"The emerald, Lanny," Rani said breathlessly. She grasped the boy's arm and shook it, Lexi style. "Is the emerald there?"

Rani quickly released Lanny's arm. He lifted the photos out of the box carefully and handed them to Isabela. Nothing else was to be found. "Well, no emerald," he said at last, "but these stills are a black-and-white treasure of movie history all by themselves."

Lexi accepted one handed to her. "What are movie stills?" she asked without thinking.

Moki whispered, "Get a clue. You just asked your brother for a definition. Do you know what you've done?"

But before Lexi could respond, Lanny said, "Stills are photos taken before and during the filming of a movie. They could be scenes from the movie, or publicity shots of the stars to advertise and promote the film."

"That's the same as pictures," Moki grumbled.

The others ignored him. Isabela's smile was as big as Lanny's.

"These are from many different movies," she said. "Tomás, look. I see our great-grandparents in most of them." Tomás took several to peruse in silence, handing each to Lanny as he finished.

Moki sighed heavily, then sat on the floor, cross-legged, as if expecting a long wait.

Lanny acted as if he were opening his own birthday present. "Wow," he said. "This one is from *City Heights*. That one is a scene from *Lost Continent*. This is from *Underground*."

"Lanny, how do you know so much about silent movies?" Isabela asked with a smile.

"As I mentioned," Lexi replied for her brother, "Lanny is a classic movie buff, Ms. de Cordoba. He feels about old Hollywood movies the way I feel about dark chocolate. You can't ever get enough."

Without taking his eyes off the stills, Lanny said, "I've seen every silent movie your great-grandparents ever made."

Next, he sorted them into piles on the floor by movie title. "Here is my favorite, *Orphans of the Swan*. And my second favorite, *Train to Paradise*. Wooow."

Isabela and Tomás were happy to let Lanny organize the stills. Moki watched, looking bored. When Lanny finished with the stacks, Moki sat up straighter. "Huh." He reached out and picked up a photo on the top of one stack, then examined it. "This one has a green paper star on its corner. See? I wonder what that means."

Rani joined Moki on the floor. The star was faded but definitely green. "What movie is the still from, Lanny?"

"*The Wedding*," he replied without hesitation.

Moki thought out loud. "The star's green . . . and emeralds are green. . . . Okay, maybe I'm crazy, but . . . does anyone else think this could be a clue to the emerald's location?"

"At a wedding?" Lexi sounded doubtful, yet she took the photo for a closer look. "Maybe an emerald wedding ring? But the emerald wasn't set into a ring. Hmm."

Lanny said, "Good going, bro, noticing the star. We need to think about this." He shuffled over and stared at the photo over Lexi's shoulder.

It was momentarily quiet, as if mental wheels were spinning in every head in the room.

Finally, Isabela broke the silence. "Well done, kids, especially you, Moki."

The boy beamed, wondering if he had finally redeemed himself in her eyes.

Lanny gathered up the other stills, taking care to keep them sorted.

Sherrill Joseph

Isabela said, "Well, no emerald yet, but we definitely have another treasure here. Let's keep this last still at the house. We can always lock it in the safe. The rest of these stills should probably go into our new safe deposit box at the bank. Tomás, yes?"

"Yeah, there's enough room for them at the bank, and they'll be secure there. Plus, my bedroom is already so overstuffed with the props from the secret room that I can hardly move."

So as not to mix in the still with the green star, Moki handed it to Isabela.

"What will you kids do while we're gone?" Tomás asked. He returned the rest of the stills to the box.

"We haven't explored the fourth level of the passages yet," Moki said.

"And Lexi and I haven't seen as much of the other passages as you guys have," Rani replied.

"Okay, so Moki, let's show the girls the passages," Lanny said. "And we four can all go together to the upper level. I want to see if that intruder might have been there. Afterwards, I think we must try to solve the next stanza of the puzzle poem before another day goes by."

"We should be back by the time you kids are done exploring the passages," Isabela said. "I'll get the poem out of the safe for you when we return from town."

Everyone agreed to the plans. The de Cordobas descended from the third floor via the house staircases with Tomás holding the latest treasure box. The four kids headed through the portrait panel and continued to the top-level passage with flashlights blazing. They scanned the cobweb-covered walls as they searched for another lever in the hopes one more door would be revealed.

"You're right, Moki." Lexi said. "This is a very cool house. Lanny, do you think we have any secret passages in *our* house?" She dodged a large spider.

"I doubt it. Our house is big, but the walls aren't thick enough to allow for passages like this place as far as I can figure. Plus, our house is old, but not this old."

"Found it," Rani said from slightly ahead of the group. She pointed to a knob protruding from a wall. "Let's see what happens when I turn it." She turned it to the right. Nothing. Then to the left. On that second try, a panel slid open. Another room. "Of course. 'Lefty loosey, righty tighty.'"

Lexi stepped into a room filled with old furniture and trunks. "Now where are we?"

Some items were draped in white sheets as they had seen in other rooms. The chamber was dead still and had not been dusted in decades. She felt as if they had gone through a time portal.

"I'd guess the attic," Moki said. "Look at that. A little stained-glass window." In three strides, he was next to it. "I can see all the way to the *casita* from here, right over the treetops. Whew. No Madame Ronescu in sight. She's probably inside there plotting whose neck she'll bite tonight. Aww!" He cupped his neck protectively with both hands.

The others busied themselves looking around the room. Lanny and Lexi poked into the trunks and other storage boxes while Rani looked for more levers. Moki returned to reality and helped, moving aside picture frames and chairs. Neither emerald nor anything else unusual was found—except for one thing.

"We didn't make all these footprints," Lanny said. He pointed to some in the dust by a far wall. "Small, as were the others we've found. Darn! I think the intruder has been searching up here, too."

Rani turned to face Lanny and almost knocked over an old lamp. "For the emerald?"

"That, and who knows what else. Let's really search and see if we can find anything."

Everyone started knocking on walls, hoping a hollow sound would reveal a panel or another secret room.

Try as they might, the squad couldn't find any more levers, buttons, panels, rooms, treasures, or the Leticia Emerald.

After a few more minutes, Lanny said, "Nothing. This is so discouraging. Let's quit here for now. Moki, you and I can show the girls the rest of the passages. That will end us up at the lions' fireplace on the first floor. Maybe the de Cordobas will be home by then, so we can check the puzzle poem."

Sometime later, the four weary, dusty explorers emerged

from the fireplace panel and found Isabela and Tomás just coming through the front door with Oso at their heels. The kids reported about the footprints they had discovered in the attic via the fourth-floor passage.

"You know," said Tomás, "it's really creepy knowing some stranger has access to our house and is taking advantage of it right under our noses."

"Well, so far, whoever it is hasn't done us physical harm," Isabela said.

"Maybe not physical harm," Rani said, brushing cobwebs from her arms, "but the intruder is searching, probably for the emerald. And theft is a violation, not to mention a crime."

"I hate to say this, but we don't know what the intruder is capable of," Lexi said.

"The best way to shut this person down," Moki said, "is to solve our mystery *wiki-wiki*."

"Yes, very quickly," Lanny replied as he gave his friend two thumbs up.

He asked Isabela for the poem, and she brought it to him from the safe. Tired, Lanny partially draped himself across the couch to read the poem stanza to the group, careful to keep his sneakers off the furniture. He respected that Isabela protected her family's antiques. Moki had already broken the leg on her bedroom footstool, and he didn't want to do anything like that in such a fine, old house.

Lexi looked on over her brother's shoulder and read out loud:

"Treehouse gardens seen from highest window stained,
Its panes have witnessed material treasures that remain
Dazzling and fine, but now hidden, soon forgotten with time,
Perhaps to be rescued because of this rhyme."

"'Treehouse gardens, highest window stained,'" Rani repeated, looking at the floor. Then she snapped her fingers. "Hey, that's what Moki said when we were in the attic. 'Treehouse gardens' might just mean that we can see over the treetops from a high place to the gardens below. 'Highest window stained' is that little stained-glass window Moki was looking out of. That's it. The attic."

"So, what are the 'material treasures' that remain and have been witnessed by the window?" Moki asked. "We've already searched the attic and couldn't find anything."

Lexi frowned. "Darn. That could mean the intruder already found them."

"'Material treasures . . . material treasures,'" Lanny said. He stared at the ceiling fresco and hugged a pillow to his chest.

"Well," Rani said, "since we've already found lots of treasures left by Lorenzo and Alondra, maybe there are more. Other than the emerald, what of theirs haven't we found yet?"

After a few seconds' pause, Lanny shot upright from the couch, and everyone shouted simultaneously, "Costumes!"

"Yes, of course. Costumes are made of fabric or 'material,'" Lanny said. "That word was meant literally, not figuratively, for a change. And costumes can be 'dazzling and fine.' You're brilliant, Rani." He jumped up and gave Rani a big hug, which she returned.

"Okay, lovebirds. Back to work," Moki said. This caused the two to blush. "The poem says they are 'now hidden.' Maybe we just need to look again. I'm all for going back to the attic. Maybe the intruder didn't have any luck the first time, either."

Lanny was all business again. "We can hope, bro." He started running for the house stairs with everyone following him up all three flights to the attic. "This reminds me of one of my favorite Sherlock Holmes stories, 'The Musgrave Ritual.' Holmes led everyone all over the house and grounds to find a missing treasure and solved the Musgrave family's ancient ritual puzzle."

"Okay, then. Lead on, Mr. Holmes," Lexi said. "But don't trip over your magnifying glass."

"Yeah, lead on, Bro Holmes," Moki said. He winked at Lexi.

"Uh, Lanny?" Rani asked. "Didn't Holmes also find a dead body in that story?"

Moki froze, causing Tomás to slam into his back. "Dead people?" Moki croaked.

"Ick," Lexi said and pretended to vomit. The others, including Lanny and Isabela, couldn't help but laugh.

"I am *not* down with that idea," Moki said.

Lanny laughed again and nudged his friend onward. "So, just how do you say 'chicken' in Hawaiian?" And once again, he had to dodge a swipe to his head from Moki.

The group finally arrived at the attic door. Isabela was the first to enter. The late afternoon sun was reflecting off a broken mirror, setting the little stained-glass window ablaze on the opposite wall. Everyone's attention was instantly drawn to it.

"That little window is really beautiful," Lexi said. She walked toward it as if hypnotized.

"I didn't notice before, but the main artistic object in that window is a tree," Lanny said. A second later, he pounded fist to palm and smiled. "That's it."

"What's 'it'?" Lexi asked.

Lanny pointed. "Look over there on that wall. What do you see?"

"A framed painting of a tree," Rani answered for Lexi. "Ah, the window was a clue."

"I get your drift, too, bro," Moki said. He dashed toward the picture.

In no time, Moki began exploring every inch of the painting with everyone watching. The frame was solidly affixed to the attic wall, unlike the moving ruby-ring portrait in the third-floor room where the movie stills had been found. But he persevered.

"Well, it won't come away from the wall," Moki said, "so there's only one thing to do." He got his fingers around the edges of the frame and started yanking and pulling on it with all his strength, causing some rattling. Isabela gasped and raised her hand to her mouth.

When Moki saw her reaction, he stopped. "Sorry. But

it just needs a little more elbow grease, Ms. de Cordoba. Really. May I please have your permission for just one teeny tiny two-person yank?"

"Well, if you really think that will do it, go ahead. Thank you for asking. But gently, gently, please." Lexi joined Moki in grabbing the corner of the frame just under where the boy was pulling.

The picture stubbornly clung to the wall, and nothing budged. Moki let out his frustration by saying some words in Hawaiian that no one asked to be translated. Apparently, they fueled his desire to succeed.

A moment later, a slight creaking sound was heard. Moki and Lexi stumbled backward as the entire wall panel released. It was hinged on the inside. Isabela gasped again, and everyone's mouths dropped open.

But they weren't shocked by the massive door.

They were shocked by what was beyond it.

CHAPTER NINETEEN

· ✧ ·

Aunt Connie Assists

"Well, just your average, everyday portrait door-knob at work," Moki said. He was the first to recover his speech.

"Wow. A hidden closet," Lexi whispered. "And it's loaded with clothes and boxes."

"OMG. 'Loaded' with a capital L," Rani replied. "Well, here are the poem's 'material treasures.'"

"Good work, bro," Lanny said. He punched his friend's arm muscle. "You, too, Lexi." Jokingly, he made a move to squeeze his sister's arm, imitating her bad habit.

"That's an understatement, Lanny," Isabela said. "Thank you so much—Moki especially. I can't believe this. What a find. You four were correct. The contents have to be our great-grandparents' costumes. These make me feel as if Tomás and I aren't so alone anymore. As if our ancestors and their love are still here at the *casa* and all around us."

Isabela gently inspected a few dresses, slowly sliding them by their hangers in order to safeguard the delicate fabrics. "Oh, look. I recognize this pale yellow dress as belonging to Great-Grandmother Alondra from her movie, *A Woman in Cairo*. Oh, and I can smell traces of the rose perfume I know was her favorite from some of her scented letters that are still part of our family's treasures. Bless you kids."

She started to bury her face in some of the garments, but pulled back just in time so as not to smear them with her bright red lipstick. The kids noticed more tears on her cheeks as she embraced each item.

After opening some boxes from the shelf above, Tomás said, "And these boots were worn by Great-Grandfather Lorenzo in his movie, *The Circus Clown*. This is way cool, beyond amazing."

"This samurai costume was worn by your great-grandfather in his movie, *Cherry Blossoms*," Lanny was quick to add. He touched it gently with a wistful look in his movie buff's eyes.

"And look at this purple-plumed hat," Isabela said. "Great-grandmother wore it in the movie *Sherwood Forest* when she played Maid Marian to Lorenzo's Robin Hood."

"There are over fifty costumes here," Moki said, "but there are gaps between some."

Rani glossed over Moki's observation in her rush to help their case. "Hey, is there a wedding dress costume?"

"Rani, of course!" Lanny said. He hit his forehead with

the heel of his hand. "You're brilliant, again." The de Cordobas stared at Lanny, not understanding his and Rani's meaning.

Lanny turned to them. "From the movie, *The Wedding*, remember?"

Rani added, "You know, the green star Moki found on the movie still for *The Wedding*?"

"Ohh, right," Isabela slowly replied. "Moki, you thought the green star from the still for that movie might be a clue to the location of the emerald."

"Well, here's a wedding dress," Lanny said in answer to Rani's question. Everyone turned to look at it as he carefully removed a delicate, long white gauzy dress from the closet by its satiny pink hanger. "This is definitely the one in the movie still."

"I say we search it," Moki said. "The emerald might be hidden on it somewhere."

"I second that search," Lexi said. Her green eyes grew large.

The task was given to Isabela. Everyone crowded around her as she carefully draped the costume across an old but relatively clean sofa. She spent ten minutes painstakingly going over every inch of the costume, feeling the fabric, squeezing the seams and hem, and inspecting the buttons, jewels, and sequins. No emerald was found. Not even a fake green stone.

As if the group wasn't disappointed enough, Moki said, "I hope the thief didn't beat us to it. I'm worried that since the costumes aren't evenly spaced on the rod, that some were taken."

"You did suggest that a few minutes ago, bro," Lanny replied. "There were footprints here besides ours, and some costumes might have been removed. But I think a thief would have ransacked the area."

"I agree with Lanny," Rani said.

"Maybe not if the thief was only after particular costumes," Moki said.

"Good point, bro," Lanny replied. "We shouldn't be too quick to assume anything. But that brings up an interesting idea—that maybe the thief knew what they were looking for. But how could that be? Hmm, this is going to take more thinking."

Lexi said, "Well, we shouldn't be so sad about not finding the emerald yet. Just look what we've found! A treasure in beautiful costumes that can now be shown to the world."

"You're right, BFF," Rani replied with a smile. "Speaking of which, we can't leave them here."

"Let's each take a load down to my room," Tomás said. "There's still some space in my closet. They should be safe there for now. I searched my room but didn't find any secret panels in the closet, and remember? The blueprints don't show any passages behind my walls." The others agreed to add the costumes to their stash of movie props in his crowded bedroom.

In no time, the entire contents of the attic closet were

carefully stowed in Tomás's room on the second floor and his door locked. The tired explorers descended to the living room. Isabela happily noticed that Moki intentionally steered clear of a delicate end table topped with an expensive vase. Tomás and the kids flopped into the plush chairs to await what smelled like a pot roast dinner being prepared by Tina. Isabela returned the puzzle poem to the wall safe, then rejoined them.

"Maybe I was wrong about the green star on the movie still," Moki said.

"I don't think so," Lexi replied. "There's got to be a connection, or the star wouldn't have been there. I'm for us keeping an eye out for things having to do with weddings."

"Not my favorite topic—weddings—but I'm in," Moki replied, grinning at Lexi.

Lexi cupped her hands over her heart, batted her eyelashes, and said, "Oh, Moki. You say the sweetest things."

Before Moki could respond, Isabela said, "I want to thank all of you for such great pieces of detective work today, uncovering both the movie stills and the costumes. But more than that, your work has given me back part of my family. And what great surprises, even if we still haven't found the emerald. I have high hopes we will yet.

"And I have another surprise for you," she added. "I've invited your aunt Connie Marlton here for dinner tonight."

Lexi leaped up. "Yay! That's right. You two met at the ARC's exhibition party."

"Yes," Isabela replied. "She's so interesting, and I asked her if we could have a preview of the photos she took of those ancient gemstones."

"Which reminds me," Lanny said. "We'll need to check in with Dr. Abbott tomorrow about the most recent gemstone thefts at the ARC."

"Good call, bro," Moki said. He slouched in his chair with his eyes closed.

"Lexi, let's go get ready for Aunt Connie's arrival," Rani said. "If there's time, Ms. de Cordoba, I'll paint some henna tattoos on your arms."

"I'd love it," the woman replied. "I think we could all use the next hour to get freshened up for our special dinner guest. Tina promises dinner will be ready on time."

The boys and Tomás stood, arched their backs with simultaneous groans, and stretched their arms to the ceiling. Then they followed the girls and Isabela, who were way ahead of them on the stairs.

Less than an hour later, the girls and their hostess descended the staircase together, looking resplendent. Lexi and Rani were dressed in the saris they had worn to the ARC party, but they had done up their hair. Rani worked a miracle getting Lexi's limp brown locks that usually straggled to her shoulders to stay pinned on top of her head.

Isabela was wearing a long, sleeveless yellow dress that showed off her dark features and newly painted reddish-brown henna tattoos. All three had put on some of Isabela's spicy perfume. The boys and Tomás had just come downstairs ahead of them and now stood frozen in their tracks, gawking at the three.

"Aren't you ladies looking especially lovely this evening," said Tomás, smiling first at the two girls, then at his sister. He took Isabela's arm to escort her into the living room.

Lanny took a cue from the pair. "Rani, you're g-g-g-gorgeous." He stumbled over his feet as he took her arm. Rani giggled and accepted his gesture.

"Lexi, you're as beautiful as a Hawaiian sunset, even if you are wearing a green Indian sari," Moki replied. He extended his arm to her.

"Oh, Moki, you're so gallant. Just like a bride-groom." Lexi said, watching his expression.

"Uh, I know you said we should watch for wedding references, but let's please take the night off from them, or I'll start perspiring in my fancy, new Hawaiian shirt."

"All in the line of duty, Moki," Lexi teased.

No sooner had everyone gotten settled in the living room when the doorbell rang. Isabela and Tomás excused themselves to greet their arriving guest. Aunt Connie's voice was heard in the entryway, and the kids ran to greet her. She barely had time to hand Isabela and Tomás a bouquet of flowers before being smothered with hugs and kisses from her detective fans.

"Whoa, let me come up for air," Aunt Connie said.

She laughed as she was jostled side to side. "This is one beautiful house," she managed to say to her host and hostess once she was able to gaze at the tiled entryway and grand staircase. "Perhaps I could photograph your estate someday. And aren't you kids lucky to get to stay here and solve a mystery?"

Lexi hung on her aunt's arm. "The only problem with staying here is we haven't had much of a chance to visit with you, Aunt Connie. And I've been wanting to tell you for the longest time that your name 'Connie' makes Rani taste cottage cheese!"

"Cottage cheese? Really? Synesthesia, huh? That's very interesting. I think your hostess figured you kids were having an 'Aunt Connie drought,' so here I am. And now I have time to hear all about your mystery and to share some of my ARC 'Gemstones of Antiquity' photos."

Tina was setting out a veggie and hummus tray on the coffee table when the group reentered the living room. As each relaxed awaiting dinner, Aunt Connie was treated to all the latest news from the kids, including the puzzle poem Isabela brought out of the safe, information about the footsteps and footprints, the secret passageways, and the treasures they had already found.

"I'm glad you kids are fearless when it comes to exploring dusty old passages," Aunt Connie said. "I've been known to do just that in order to take a special photograph."

"Yes, it's fun and exciting," Lexi replied with a fist pump.

Her friends nodded.

The party soon moved into the dimly-lit dining room where the twinkling table candles made the silverware and crystal shimmer. Moki copied Lexi and placed his large cloth napkin across his lap. A scrumptious pot roast dinner was served and eaten before the conversation about the estate's mysterious happenings had concluded.

Tina placed thick slices of chocolate fudge layer cake with ample scoops of mint-chip ice cream in front of each guest.

"We are certainly fortunate to have you four detectives on the case," Isabela said. "Tomás and I have been amazed at your skills in uncovering our great-grandparents' movie memorabilia."

Moki sighed as he forked up bites of his second slice of cake. "Yeah, but still no emerald."

"Bro, I have lots of hope we'll find the emerald yet," Lanny replied with thumbs up.

Aunt Connie dabbed her mouth with her napkin. "Which reminds me. Don't let me leave without sharing with all of you after dinner some of the photographs I took at the ARC gemstone preview party the other night."

"Cool that we get to see them ahead of the rest of the world, before you publish them in the International Geographic Institute's magazine," Rani said. Her many brass bracelets jangled as if singing her excitement.

Aunt Connie patted Rani's henna-tattooed hand. "Yes, and even ahead of Dr. Abbott. But remember. Only a few of the finest photos will actually make it into the journal. Maybe all of you can help me decide which will make the cut."

Everyone, including Moki, had finished eating. The kids led the way to the living room to see the photographs. Aunt Connie lifted a thick stack of photos from her briefcase and wiggled her way between the twins in the middle of the sofa in order to share and explain each photo effectively to the entire group. Isabela and Tomás pulled up closely in nearby chairs.

"Look at the beautiful markings in that lapis stone," Lexi said about one photo. "You really captured the details there to bring out its beauty. That's because you're such a fab photog."

"Thanks, Lexi." She shared many more pictures, each seemingly more striking than the last.

"These are some gorgeous pictures, Aunt Connie," Moki said. He took care to touch them only around the edges. "All these look great. How will you weed them out?"

"Thanks, Moki. There are ways to cull them. For instance, some shots are too distant. They may look interesting, but we mostly want to go for details when it comes to gemstones. I took some just for fun. Like this one." She handed a photo to him.

"Ha! There's Moki stuffing his face with brownies," Lanny said. He tipped backward with laughter against the sofa cushion. "That's rich. Make that your journal cover, Aunt Connie."

Moki elbowed Lanny in his ribs. "No. That photo and its negative must die."

"And here's one with some guests in the photo, but one person looks fuzzy," Rani said. "See? She's in the background. It definitely distracted me from the rest of the shot." Rani pointed to a figure wearing something glittery and black by the dessert buffet.

"Yeah. It looks like a caterer photobombed the shot, Auntie C," Lexi said.

"Yes, I noticed that, too," said Aunt Connie. "Good eyes, you two. Scratch that photo."

But something had caught Isabela's eye. "May I see that, please?" Connie handed her the photo. Isabela's smile slowly faded and her eyebrows knitted together more intensely the longer she stared at it.

"What's wrong, sis?" Tomás's attention shifted to the figure as well.

Isabela kept her gaze trained on the photo's subject. Sparks seemed to shoot from her eyes. "I know this person in the background."

CHAPTER TWENTY

· ✧ ·

Lantern in the Churchyard

"**I**t's Cousin Olivia!" Isabela shouted. Her gaze left the photo and met her brother's.

"But that can't be." He took Aunt Connie's photo from Isabela's hand. "Cousin Olivia's in Europe. Surely she would have told us if she'd returned to the States, no?"

"Whether or not she'd inform us of her travel plans doesn't change the fact that that's still Olivia," Isabela said. She jabbed her finger at the image in the photo. "Her face looks a bit different, but you can't mistake her with her dark features and upswept hairdo. And the sparkly black top she's wearing? It was a birthday gift from me."

Lanny asked, "Why would your cousin attend the ARC party in the first place, even come out into the open, but not come forward to say hello to you, Ms. de Cordoba?"

"Olivia left California and this house with bad feelings. But how those feelings and actions connect to her strange appearance and behavior at the party are baffling to me."

Tomás sighed deeply. "Yes, that's Olivia, all right. All this does seem inexplicable."

"What can be explained," Lanny replied, "is that your cousin had some purpose for being at the ARC even if we don't know yet what it was. And apparently, she was testing you to see if you would recognize her, which you didn't—until now."

"And we also know she wasn't there to help the caterers," Rani added seriously. "She's not wearing a uniform as are the others."

Moki shrugged his shoulders. "Wow. So, now we have one mystery here and two at the ARC. I hope our detective abilities live up to our new reputation."

"Just think, everyone," Lexi said. "If Ms. de Cordoba hadn't invited Aunt Connie here tonight, and if she hadn't shared her photos with us, we wouldn't have this valuable clue. Thanks, Ms. de Cordoba and Aunt Connie."

"And maybe your cases are linked somehow," Aunt Connie suggested offhandedly.

Lanny breezed over his aunt's comment. "How do you know it's a valuable clue?"

Lexi smirked. "How do you know it isn't? And Aunt Connie might be right."

"True enough. And a detective must consider all angles—all ideas and all clues, good or bad." Lanny returned her smirk.

"Say, does Olivia have a key to this house?" Rani asked. "She used to live here, right?"

"Yes, but I changed the locks after she left because she seemed hostile toward us." Isabela sighed. "I felt it was the safe thing to do at the time. Now, I'm glad I did it."

"Something else changed—and not for the better," Tomás said. "Olivia wasn't herself when she left here. She was so negative after her parents died last year, which was understandable, but she refused to get help for her anger. No telling what her troubles could have gotten her into."

Without warning, the living room's French doors flew wide open with a bang, and everyone jumped. Strong, bracing winds crashed into the room, sending Aunt Connie's photographs flying.

"Quick," she said. "Grab the pictures before they disappear into the night."

Everyone scrambled, and in no time, all her photos were accounted for, the doors secured, and the room straightened. The sudden activity had mellowed the previous, serious discussion.

"I think that's my cue to leave," the photographer said and turned to her hosts. "Could be a storm brewing. I want to get home to Quince Street before it hits. I'll say good night, and I'm sorry about your cousin. But thank you for an otherwise lovely evening."

At the front door, Connie hugged the de Cordobas and the kids.

Lexi smiled. "Thanks again, Aunt Connie, for sharing the photos and for helping our case."

Everyone walked the twins' aunt to her car while eyeing the dark, wispy clouds scudding across the moonless sky. The cool winds were now wuthering relentlessly through the estate's mature trees, swirling leaves, and causing the wind chimes on the front porch to clang wildly.

As the photographer drove off down the street, the others scurried to get back indoors where it was warm and bright. Tomás turned to his sister and to cheer her said, "Bet you five bucks we get a downpour tonight."

Isabela read his strategy. "You're on. I think the winds will blow the clouds off this time. We don't usually get rain in Las Palmitas in September. That storm the other night was fluky."

"Get your money ready, sis," Tomás replied. He winked at the kids as everyone continued walking. Once inside, they plodded up the stairs, leaving the winds to rage outside. The subject of Olivia was obviously closed for the night. Everyone followed Tomás's lead and was soon fast asleep.

At two a.m., a knocking sound woke Lexi and caused her to sit bolt upright in bed. She strained to look around the room. The bedroom window had come unlatched by the high winds and was banging against the outside wall. Rani had somehow managed to sleep through the racket.

"Aww, darn that window," Lexi whispered. She crawled over her disheveled pile of bed covers, then tiptoed as quickly as possible to fix the problem. It took a couple of tries to grab ahold of the window before she succeeded in latching it. Rani mumbled and fidgeted in the other bed.

Lexi was about to turn toward Rani when she became transfixed by something she saw out the troublesome window. At the far western edge of the estate grounds, there appeared a light that seemed to be bobbing, then pulsing on and off. Lexi squinted her eyes to aid her focus.

"What's going on?" Rani asked a moment later. She propped herself up on her elbows.

"There's a twinkling light out there. Come see for yourself." Lexi beckoned to Rani with both hands. "Hurry up, before it's gone."

Rani scrambled out of bed and joined Lexi in gazing in the direction her friend was pointing. Both girls watched as the light moved first one direction, then the other.

Rani craned her neck for a better view. "Creepy. What part of the garden is that?"

"I hope I'm wrong, but I think that's the churchyard at St. Barnabas Cathedral."

The girls stared at each other wide-eyed as Lexi squeezed Rani's forearm.

After returning to watch the light for another minute, Lexi said, "There. The light's standing still now. I bet it's a lantern, and someone has stopped to search for something."

Rani shivered. "Spooky. What could they be looking for in the dead of night in a cemetery? Uh, sorry. Poor choice of words. On second thought, don't answer that question."

"It's clearly in the churchyard, though. I wonder what's making the light appear to flicker on and off. Could it be a signal?"

"Maybe, but I think it's more likely that the wind is to blame. The trees and bushes between the lantern and us are being blown around, probably causing the light to appear to flash on and off."

"Yeah. That makes sense, BFF. Do you think the guys are awake watching this, too?" Lexi asked.

"Well, even if they're awake, they wouldn't be watching it. Their room isn't angled the way ours is, so they don't have the same view."

"Oh, right. But back to the matter of what the person is searching for," Lexi said. She noticed her teeth chattering, and she was certain it wasn't just from the chilly night air.

Rani grabbed Lexi's shoulders. "I know I'm going to hate myself for suggesting this, but how about if we find out?"

It only took Lexi a second to reply. "You're on, girlfriend. Let's get dressed."

The girls clambered into dark clothes, grabbed their unlit flashlights, and tiptoed as quickly as possible downstairs.

Once on the first floor, Rani whispered, "Let's use the kitchen door. It's closest to where we're going."

"Got it," Lexi replied and led the way past the stove. The humming refrigerator seemed somehow reassuring.

First, she disabled the alarm system using the code Isabela had given them. Then, she turned the service porch doorknob slowly to avoid losing control of the door if the powerful winds happened to catch it.

Lexi glanced up at the starry but cloud-speckled sky. "No moon to light our way."

"All the better to camouflage us," Rani replied. She pulled on the ties of her windbreaker hood to cover her head and ears sufficiently. "We'll see Lantern Person, but they won't see us."

"Right. I love having the element of surprise," Lexi said with twinkling eyes.

"Looks as if Ms. de Cordoba wins the bet with her brother," Rani said. "No rain."

"Yay. That means no mud, just wind. Works for me."

The pair made their way slowly toward the low stone wall that formed the boundary between the de Cordoba property and that of the cathedral. They were thankful for the din of the strong winds through the trees that covered any noise they made as they brushed against many shrubs and branches. When the girls finally reached the churchyard and crouched down behind the wall, they no longer saw the light. Their brief detective experience told them to wait patiently.

They weren't disappointed. A minute later, Lexi tugged on Rani's sleeve and whispered, "Look! There's the light again. Lantern Person is coming back into view."

"Yeah, and look where from—from behind the de Cordoba family's humongous mausoleum. The person is circling it and definitely looking for something there."

The girls watched the activity for a few more minutes, debating about what to do next, when the decision was made for them. The winds had caused a dry branch of an old pine tree to snap off, topple into the churchyard, and whack a headstone near where the girls hid. A startled Lexi let out a muffled scream, but it proved loud enough to attract the searcher.

Lantern Person set out at full speed, leaping over headstones and then the wall, not looking back. The girls immediately pursued the mysterious figure, who was apparently heading for the far southern part of the de Cordoba's property. The lantern glowed no more.

"That's where Madame Ronescu lives," Lexi said breathlessly. "Let's go."

"I hope Lantern Person doesn't know we know that," Rani said. She was glad she and Lexi knew the grounds well, or they could have gotten tangled or lost among the foliage. They successfully dodged trees and ducked behind bushes to avoid being detected by the speedy intruder.

After a few minutes' chase, Rani suddenly pulled her friend to a stop. "Lexi, it's clear to me where Lantern Person is going. Let's quit running and take a shortcut through the gardens. We can stake out the *casita* and see what happens."

"Fab idea," Lexi replied. "Let's see what's so special about Madame Ronescu's place."

In no time, the girls were hidden in a high, thick oleander bush that gave them an excellent view of the *casita* entrance about twenty feet ahead. Within two minutes, Lantern Person, dark-haired and dressed in black, arrived as Rani had hoped, looked around quickly, knocked softly but rapidly on the cottage door, and was unceremoniously yanked inside. The door banged shut, and the girls heard the lock snap in place.

"Wow. You were right, Rani. Now what?" Lexi did not take her eyes off the door.

"Do you remember that day when we inspected the grounds with Ms. de Cordoba after the rainstorm?" Rani asked. "One of the shutters on a *casita* window had come off. Let's go see if we can peek through. Maybe the people inside forgot to close the curtains."

"I'm in. Let's go." Lexi pushed her friend forward.

The girls emerged from their hiding place and hurried across the lawn. The raging winds muffled the sound of their footsteps. More luck. The shutter was still lying against the cottage's outer wall. They silently approached the window. Luck was still on their side. The curtains carelessly gaped open in the center, so the girls could see inside by taking turns.

Lexi's eyes bulged out at the sight. There stood Lantern Person, a woman. And with her was a much younger version of Madame Ronescu, who was sitting with a crumpled dress, made from many yards of fabric, on her lap. Despite the winds, the girls could make out the women's loud, angry discussion.

"I keep telling you I didn't find anything in the churchyard," said Lantern Person. She gripped the back of a nearby chair. "A couple of kids saw me, but fortunately, I lost them in the dark." Lexi and Rani turned and smiled at each other.

"It's just got to be there," the seated woman replied. She stabbed her needle and thread into a pincushion on the end table. "Those snoopy kids staying with your cousins must have been out spying again. They're supposedly amateur detectives. We better keep our eyes on them. Now look. I've finished working on the last batch of dresses you brought. Hide this one until we can smuggle it out of here."

She thrust into Lantern Person's arms what appeared to be an old pink brocade costume. As Lantern Person took it, the *casita's* firelight played across the fabric.

Lexi and Rani stared at one another. Could it be?

The costume was ablaze with sparkling gemstones.

CHAPTER TWENTY-ONE

· ✧ ·

Glittering Exposé

"Thanks for the homemade breakfast quesadilla," Moki said to a yawning Lexi. The girls had joined the boys behind a small grove of trees within sight of the *casita*. "I thought I was going to have to eat some of these green bananas," he added as he pointed to the fruit overhead. Moki had on a thick neck scarf, more to protect himself from Madame Ronsecu than from the nonexistent cold.

Lexi said, "Just wanted to say thanks to you and Lanny for staking out the *casita* after Rani and I returned to the house last night to get some sleep." She yawned again.

"No problem," Lanny said. "You girls probably solved our ARC gemstone theft case with your spying on Cousin Olivia and Madame Ronescu last night." He briefly set aside his binoculars to eat.

Rani handed the guys juice boxes and said, "Something's weird about that. The person inside the *casita* looked like Madame Ronescu, except thirty years younger.

Lantern Person, however, was obviously Cousin Olivia. The Madame Ronescu woman commented about us 'snoopy kids' staying with Lantern Person's *cousins*."

Lexi said, "And unfortunately, Lantern Person did resemble the woman in Aunt Connie's photo." She sighed. "It's so sad for Ms. de Cordoba and Tomás. Their family keeps shrinking. Maybe there is a 'Green Curse' after all."

Rani's eyes were downcast. "I don't know about a curse, but it's certainly a tragedy. I must admit, your aunt's photos did help me recognize Cousin Olivia last night and also some of the ARC jewels sewn onto the dress."

"Has anyone left the *casita* yet?" Lexi asked. She strained to see between the banana leaves.

"No action yet," Moki replied. He downed large bites of his breakfast. "That's good for us. It will give my dad time to get here with a search warrant for the place."

Lanny shrugged. "I hate to mention it, but one or both of the women could have left after you girls returned to the house last night to get Moki and me."

"I've been wondering what Lantern Person, aka Cousin Olivia, was searching for around the mausoleum," Lexi said. "And that Madame Ronescu person saying, 'It just had to be there.'"

"Hopefully, we'll find out soon," Rani replied. "Last night's adventure could explain how the daisies got trampled. Maybe Cousin Olivia was searching there some other time and got spooked."

The detectives' whispered conversation continued for

another half hour. Moki's dad still hadn't arrived, and they heard no sounds from inside the *casita*.

"I'm concerned that what Lanny said might be true," Moki said. "Maybe they *are* gone."

"Then let's find out," Rani said. "Come on." She emerged from behind the tree grove and smoothed her rumpled shorts after grabbing a small bag. The others joined her, not sure of the plan, as she marched up to the front door of the *casita* and knocked loudly. Moki grabbed his neck, repositioned his scarf, and motioned for them to run.

After a full minute of more knocking, the door slowly opened. There stood the same elderly Madame Ronescu, whom they had first met, still stooped over and clutching her cane.

"What do you want?" she asked with a scowl and thick Romanian accent while blocking the kids' view into the house.

With a bright smile, Rani said, "Madame Ronescu, *bună dimineaţa. Eşti o vrăjitoare.*"

"Huh?" she replied after a momentary pause. Her face had clearly paled.

Rani repeated the phrase.

"Oh, uh, I speak only English in America," Madame Ronescu said. "I ask you again. What do you want?"

"We just wanted to bring you these pears from Ms. de Cordoba's garden." Rani pushed a small paper bag of fruit into Madame Ronescu's gloved hands. "Have a nice day."

The kids turned away before she could reply and strolled back toward the garden near where they had been hiding. After getting some distance away, Lexi said, "Rani, you were incredible. We now know at least one person is still inside. But what did you say to her?"

Rani giggled. "I said, 'Good morning. You are a witch,' in Romany."

Moki's eyebrows hiked. "How did you learn how to say that?"

"Googled it," she replied as she buffed her fingernails on her shirt.

Lanny snapped his fingers. "But what's more important is Madame Ronescu didn't understand what Rani said, which means—"

"Which means she's an imposter, a phony, a fake with a capital F," a grinning Rani said.

"But we haven't yet ruled out a vampiress," Moki said.

Everyone rolled their eyes.

After another fifteen minutes had passed, the kids decided the boys would continue the stakeout while the girls would leave to check around the mausoleum. Six adults approached, which ended their plans. Oso trotted a few paces behind them.

Moki ran to greet his father, Sergeant Dan, and the officer's partner Sergeant Yolanda Osuna. "Did you get the search warrant, Dad?" the boy asked. His pride in his father showed on his face.

"We certainly did." He waved it in front of Moki.

Isabela stood near the officers. "I'm not prepared for what we might find in the *casita*. I doubt that I ever could be." She looked helplessly at Tomás, who supported her with his arm. "To think our cousin could be a thief. And the woman I rented a home to right here on our own property might be her accomplice."

Oso seemed to sense his owner's anxiety and rubbed against her leg affectionately.

Dr. Abbott stepped forward and shook his head. "This whole turn of events makes me deeply regret that I ever arranged to have the gemstone exhibit at the ARC."

Mr. Dayton stood next to the director and said, "I'm sorry now, too. But if you kids have really found the stolen gemstones, my company and I will be most grateful." He dabbed at his sweaty forehead with a handkerchief.

"Recovering the gems could well be the only good thing that comes from this," Dr. Abbott said.

It was now almost a half hour after the kids gave Madame Ronescu the fruit. The large group walked toward the front door of the cottage but maintained a safe distance away as Sergeant Dan instructed. He and Sergeant Osuna approached and knocked loudly.

"This is the police," he said. "I have a search warrant. Open the door—now."

"You have no business here," Madame Ronescu said fiercely from behind the locked door.

"I repeat. I have a warrant to search the premises. Open

the door, or we will have to enter forcibly."

Shrieks were suddenly heard from inside the *casita* followed by string of words, not in Romany, but in French. As the door slowly opened, the two officers noticed a young woman rapidly descending a drop-down staircase from the attic. Seeing the officers, she tried to bolt past them, but Sergeant Osuna caught her arm and held her securely. "Let me go. Let me go!" she shouted.

"Oh, Cousin Olivia!" Isabela cried as she approached the squirming woman. "What have you gotten yourself into?"

Olivia turned and looked her cousin in the eye. Instead of the smirk Isabela was expecting, Olivia shook from genuine confusion and fright.

Before Olivia could answer, the person who had called herself Madame Ronescu and had posed as an elderly Rom emerged from behind the door. The kids gasped. The woman standing upright before them was now thirty years younger. Her clothing was fashionable and expensive-looking. Her raggedy head scarf and gray hair had vanished. Instead, dark hair fell loosely to her shoulders. The heavy makeup, wrinkles, and cane were gone as well. The transformation was incredible. Suitcases sat nearby. Apparently, the two women had planned to leave town that morning and had certainly not anticipated being caught by either the kids or the de Cordobas, let alone the police.

"Madame Rouchard, what should we do?" Olivia shouted. "I don't want to go to jail."

"Shut your mouth, silly girl," the older woman said, now with a French accent. "They have nothing on us."

"Madame Rouchard, not Ronescu?" Sergeant Dan asked.

"Yes, that's her real name," Olivia said. "Celeste Rouchard. If I tell you everything, will you let me go? She's the real criminal, wanted for multiple jewel thefts across Europe. She planned everything. She made me help."

The girls glanced at Isabela, who appeared haggard and spent over this new family tragedy. Even her usual careful grooming couldn't erase her look of defeat.

"You both have the right to remain silent . . ." Sergeant Dan began.

"Don't worry, *Monsieur Policeman*. The only thing I will say, other than the fact that Olivia is not *Mademoiselle Innocent*, is I want to see a lawyer." Her lips pinched shut.

"And that can be arranged at police headquarters," Sergeant Dan said. "But first, we will search this house. Here's the warrant." He pushed it into her hands. Both women were soon handcuffed.

Olivia screamed, "Please, I don't want to go to jail! I'll tell you everything."

Isabela patted her cousin's shoulder. "Olivia," she said quietly, "try to calm yourself. You must go with them now. You can tell your story at police headquarters. Tomás and I will find a way to help you. And try not to worry."

The kids were impressed but not surprised by Isabela's generosity.

Sergeant Dan said, "Do either of you women care to make it easier on yourselves in the long run by telling us now where you've hidden the gemstones that I strongly suspect are inside the cottage?"

Olivia started to speak, but it wasn't necessary. Oso had sneaked into the *casita* and was now pawing at a window seat compartment. Lexi walked over and lifted the seat. There in a rumpled heap was the pink dress she and Rani had seen the night before. Three other costumes had also been stuffed inside. Last was the cassette tape that Lanny had suspected was removed from the old recorder.

"Come see the great work Detective Oso has done," Lexi said. She held up the items as she and Rani removed them from their hiding place. Sunshine streaming through the window lit up the clothing.

"That's the pink dress from your great-grandparents' movie, *Sunset Fantasy*," Lanny said to Isabela and Tomás. "And look how it sparkles. Those aren't just sequins sewn on the front."

"You're correct, Lanyon," Dr. Abbott said. He smiled and rubbed his hands together.

Chris Dayton got busy counting and authenticating the stones on all the costumes that he spread out on a table. Soon, his face lit up. "And they're *all* here." Then, he exhaled deeply.

"See? Madame Rouchard sewed all those jewels onto the costumes," Olivia said.

"Costumes *you* stole from the house," Madame

Rouchard replied. "Now, close your mouth, girl, or I'll be telling them everything about you."

Lexi thought it was the cold, penetrating look in Madame Rouchard's eyes that linked this French woman to the Rom she had impersonated.

Rani bent down more closely to see the stones that had been expertly sewn on in elaborate patterns. They blended perfectly into each costume. She whistled. "It isn't just gold that glitters."

Isabela turned to her cousin. "Olivia, how did you find out about the passages in the house?"

Olivia stared at the ground. "I ordered a copy of the house's blueprints from the county recorder's office. My parents told me stories about the passages. The blueprints confirmed their existence. I had to use those passages after I returned from Europe and discovered my house key no longer worked. I had to get in somehow. I didn't think I'd be welcome anymore after the way I talked to you and Tomás before I left. Plus, Celeste Rouchard and I knew the ancient gemstones were coming to Las Palmitas. She—" At this point, Olivia burst into tears and could say no more. Isabela embraced her.

Lexi and Moki joined Rani, who was now snuggling with Oso in the *casita*. "So, Rani, what does the name 'Rouchard' make you taste? The same thing as 'Ronescu'?" Moki asked quietly.

"No, something different. 'Rouchard' is the scorched insides of a jack-o-lantern."

"Eww! You've actually eaten that?" Moki asked as he backed away from her.

"No. But I've smelled it, so I can still experience its taste."

"Which proves your synesthesia has once again helped us solve the case," he said.

"How?" Rani asked. "The two names don't give me the same taste."

"But both names, Ronescu and Rouchard, taste nasty to you. And like in our first case where this also happened, we had one bad guy pretending to be another bad guy."

She glanced suspiciously at him. "You do have an active imagination, Moki."

"Well, I can imagine, too," said Lexi, "and right now, I'm imagining what's in store for Cousin Olivia and Madame Celeste. And it will be even nastier."

CHAPTER TWENTY-TWO

· ✧ ·

Clues from Old Hollywood

The two thieves, stolen gems, missing cassette tape, and four costumes headed to police headquarters. Isabela and Tomás, despite feeling devastated by the tragic turn of events, went along to see if there was anything they could do for their cousin. Isabela planned to call her new friend, Troy Landis, to see if he could recommend a good criminal lawyer.

Dr. Abbott and Mr. Dayton thanked the kids profusely again and returned to the ARC after identifying each stone for the police report. The men were pleased that the gems had been recovered even though the stones would remain in police custody for a while as evidence during the women's trials.

Lexi lightly punched her brother's shoulder. "So, our cases on Eucalyptus Street and at the ARC were connected after all, just as Aunt Connie suggested."

"Yes. I stand corrected. So, next, we need to search

around the mausoleum now. That emerald has to be somewhere on the grounds," Lanny replied.

"Well, what are we waiting for?" asked Rani. She headed off toward the churchyard.

Moki peeled off his neck scarf. "Yeah, let's go tromp around the tombstones. 'Countess Dracula' will be behind bars soon, so my neck is safe again."

The four kids entered the churchyard. Fortunately, for privacy's sake, they were the only visitors. They circled the mausoleum many times as Olivia had done. They scanned the walls and high, barred window at the back, scoured the ground around the entire perimeter, and inspected the locked iron door. Forty-five minutes passed. They found nothing out of the ordinary. Certainly not the emerald.

"We need the puzzle poem," Lanny finally said. "We only have one more stanza to decipher. That's got to lead us to the emerald."

"But the de Cordobas are at the police station," Rani replied. "The poem's in the safe."

Lanny looked at the squad. "Then does anyone remember what the last stanza said?"

Lexi shook her head. "Something about 'blackened roses' and 'Gray's elegy' are all I recall. I don't see any blackened roses here, though this would be a likely spot for some."

"Hey, guys, what about the green star on the movie still?" Moki asked. "Don't forget that."

"Great reminder, bro." Lanny gave Moki a thumbs

up. "I think if we put the poem and the movie still together, we just might have some luck."

As the kids stood thinking about what to do next, Lexi's phone rang. "It's Ms. de Cordoba," Lexi said. She answered the call.

Isabela was reporting that she and Tomás had returned home from police headquarters. Tina had made lunch, and the kids were invited to come back to the house to eat. She felt all of them could use a break after today's sad events.

Lexi replied for the group, "We're on the way," then shared the invitation with her friends.

"Yay, food," Moki said. "Best excuse I know of to leave this place." He took large strides to exit the church-yard and led the gallop through the gardens toward the house.

"Not that you needed an excuse," Lanny yelled from a few yards behind.

Lexi hugged herself as she followed. "I'm not looking forward to seeing the de Cordobas' faces after they witnessed their only relative being booked on suspicion of grand theft."

"We'll just have to do what we can to cheer them up," Rani said.

The others nodded.

Lexi said, "The good news is, with Cousin Olivia and Madame Celeste behind bars, our competition for the emerald is gone. And let's not forget we've solved the ARC gemstone case."

"You're right," Rani replied. "Now, we can focus on finding the emerald." She gave Lexi a high-five.

From the back of the caravan, Lanny said, "And let's not forget that the first stanza of the poem indicated 'the ending is at the start.' We'll need to look at that stanza again, too."

"Okay, but after lunch, bro," Moki said.

The group bounded into the house through the French doors. Moki inhaled deeply. "I smell tacos." In his excitement about food, Moki flung his hands wildly, accidentally hitting a large vase as he stormed into the dining room. The object tilted and started to fall to the hardwood floor. Rani scrambled to catch it, but Isabela got there first. She did a half-twist and pulled the vase into her body with both hands. The object was saved!

After a few seconds to still her racing heart and on the brink of tears, she said with a cracking voice, "Moki, Moki, Moki, what am I going to do with you?"

Beads of perspiration gleamed on the boy's forehead. "I'm so sorry, Ms. de Cordoba. I guess I can't take myself anywhere. So, if you have a dungeon, maybe that's the safest place for me."

Moki had not intended to be funny, but the other kids started laughing. They quickly tried to stop themselves, not sure if it was appropriate after the sad events of the morning. Isabela stared at the kids. Tomás started to chuckle, which set the kids off again. Then she, too, burst out laughing, doubled over while still hugging the vase, and outdid the other five combined. Isabela's nerves had become unstrung over Olivia, and a hearty laugh right this moment was just the cure.

Bless Moki and his gift for comic relief, they all thought.

Isabela brushed some salty tears off her face. "Come on, Moki. No dungeon, just a dining room. Eat as much as you like. And I won't even mind if you don't use your napkin today."

Moki was speechless and decided he'd use a napkin, anyway.

Once the kids had washed their hands and returned to the dining room, Isabela personally assisted Moki into his chair.

✧

An hour later, after a pleasant lunch together, everyone was determined to focus on the positive. Lexi often said that in tough times, looking on the bright side is what courageous people do. The detectives tried to act on that idea frequently.

Lanny smoothed the puzzle poem out on the dining room table and bent over it. The rest of the squad and the de Cordobas surrounded him.

"I'm for finding that emerald today," Lanny said. His broad smile was mirrored by all.

Lexi read the last stanza out loud:

*"At the end of it all, blackened roses, wicked thorns, and
    delusions,*
*So from Gray's elegy, I ask if beauty isn't wasted in
    seclusion?*
*Searching must continue now but at a funeral's pace,
    awaiting the light*
*That appears however improbably, yet shining green and
    eternally bright."*

"'At the end of it all,'" Rani said. "Maybe that means the end of the poem."

"Or the end of our search," Moki replied.

"Or the end of life—death," Lexi said.

Everyone stood bolt upright and looked one to the other.

"I think it could mean all three," Lanny said. "Remember what Lexi said earlier, that the mausoleum would be a likely spot for dying things?"

"Yeah, I can picture roses left after a funeral," Lexi replied. "They would eventually wither and turn black, and their thorns would get exposed. And 'delusions' might mean that sometimes people die before they've realized all their dreams."

"As far as I'm concerned, there are too many dead things in that stanza," Moki said.

Rani said quickly, "I think that you're on to something, Lexi. Check out the next part. We studied that line from Gray's elegy with Bruce. He said sometimes people die and are forgotten, or their talents go unnoticed because those abilities were hidden or secluded."

EUCALYPTUS STREET: GREEN CURSE

"Man, in this case, that's got to mean the emerald," Moki said. "It's beautiful and hidden, all right."

"And here's proof positive Great-Grandfather Lorenzo really wanted the emerald found," said Isabela, "because next he said the search 'must continue.'"

"And it's been at a 'funeral's pace,' all right," Rani said, "because we had to solve all the previous stanzas and discover the rest of the treasures first." She gave a little jump of excitement.

Lexi was almost breathless. "Plus 'funeral's pace' is another clue pointing us to the mausoleum." She looked around for someone's arm to squeeze, but everyone backed away.

Lanny gave a tongue click. "It certainly sounds funereal to me."

Moki cocked his head. "Fune—what, Professor Lexicon? Oh, shoot. I did it again."

"It means *pertaining to a funeral*," Lanny said. He crossed his eyes at Moki.

"In that case, your word—along with that stanza— need to be laid to rest," Moki said. The girls moaned.

"But why 'awaiting the light'?" Lanny asked. He often ignored Moki's teasing after "word lessons."

"And how can light be 'improbable'?" Rani asked.

"Because . . . light doesn't . . . normally shine . . . inside . . . your typical mausoleum," Lexi said. She snapped her fingers. "So, we have to wait for some light source is my guess."

Tomás shrugged his shoulders and casually said, "The de Cordoba mausoleum has a high window."

"Ha! Of course. That's it!" Lanny said. The heel of his hand met his head. "The light from the window will show us the emerald that is 'shining green and eternally bright.'"

"But where exactly is the emerald?" Moki asked. "I'm not digging around inside any mausoleum. Oops. I didn't mean that the way it came out."

"Don't worry, Moki," Isabela replied." I doubt Great-Grandfather Lorenzo would have had the emerald buried inside his or any relative's coffin. He was dramatic but far from morbid."

"I'm counting on your being right about that, Ms. de Corboda," he said.

"Moki, you told us not to forget the movie still with the green star," Rani said. "I say we focus on that clue now that we've solved the last stanza."

"Another one of your many good ideas, Rani," Lanny said. He appreciated her effectiveness at keeping them on track, not losing any threads or important clues.

"I'll get the still from the wall safe," Isabela said and left the room.

"While we're waiting, why don't we look at the first stanza again?" Lanny asked as he pointed to it on the sheet of paper. "The last two lines of this stanza say,

To find what you seek, you must dash and dart

Only to discover that the ending was at the start.

Moki replied, "Yeah, and the first two lines say,

Wishful dreams of bold emerald trappings
From radiant treetop and archaic wrappings."

"It seems obvious to me now," Rani said. "'Bold emerald trappings' means the emerald is decorating something, and 'wishful dreams' is that we want to find the gem."

"But 'radiant treetop' . . ." Lexi added. "A living tree? Not likely inside a mausoleum."

"Agreed," Tomás replied. "But there are trees in the cemetery outside the mausoleum."

"True," Lanny said. "And 'archaic wrappings' . . . could refer to old burial clothes."

"Oh, no," said Moki. "It's sounding more and more to me as if we have to dig." He wrapped his arms around his neck.

"Well, since we're stumped about the tree—ha, ha—I say we think about the movie still," Lanny said. His friends groaned as Isabela handed him the photo. "Ideas?" he asked them.

"I say we should watch the movie *The Wedding* and see if we get a clue," Rani said.

"You keep coming up with brilliant suggestions," Lanny said. "I'll get it on my phone."

"I have another idea," Isabela said. "I haven't seen that movie in ages. How about if I make some popcorn and we watch it on our home movie screen? I have it on DVD."

Thumbs up all around. Lanny was glad that, despite the de Cordobas' focus on the past, at least they believed in technology. Moki was just happy there would be snacks.

Isabela led the group to what she called the movie room. The kids couldn't believe what they were seeing. It was actually an old gilded theatre with scents of popcorn and candy lingering from bygone days. In no time, the group, including Oso, was gathered in front of the theatre-sized screen. Everyone settled into a plush velvet seat, and the lights faded to blackness.

Lanny barely ate any of the buttery snack, mesmerized by the film. There was Alondra in the wedding gown they had found in the attic closet. And Lorenzo appeared in a tuxedo also found among those treasures. Isabela and Tomás exchanged many smiles as they watched their great-grandparents' performances. An hour passed. No clue.

Or so they thought.

Immediately as the movie ended, Lanny jumped to his feet and snapped his fingers.

"Guys, I know where the emerald is!"

CHAPTER TWENTY-THREE

· ✧ ·

The Key from St. Barnabas

I t was no use trying to stop Lanny to get an explanation following the movie. He led the charge to the cemetery with the others running to catch up. Soon, the boy stood under the barred mausoleum window. Isabela confirmed the bars had been added by Lorenzo in the late 1940s, though she didn't know why. Next, Lanny ran to the mausoleum's door and pulled on its iron ring.

"It can only be opened with a key," Tomás said as Lanny continued to tug on the handle. "St. Barnabas Cathedral's monsignor has it."

"I'll go find Father Pete," Isabela said. "From the organ music, I'd say he's inside the cathedral." She darted off. Lanny stayed by the door, pacing and deep in thought. He didn't notice that the others including Tomás had wandered over to inspect around the jacaranda tree. After a few minutes, however, the three kids rejoined Lanny at the door.

"Okay, bro," Moki said. "While we wait, what was the clue you saw during the movie?"

"No one else saw it?" he asked. "It was during the fade-out scene. Remember? Alondra's and Lorenzo's characters had just gotten married in the church. There was a stained-glass window in front of them, which they faced. Then, they turned back toward the camera and smiled. Didn't you notice any of that?"

"I was pretty much focused on the bride and groom only," Rani replied.

"Me, too," Lexi said.

"So, what exactly did you see, bro?" Moki asked. He sighed with impatience.

Lanny clutched his hair with both hands. "Aww! The window, bro. The window! And the tree. But Ms. de Cordoba needs to return before the sun sets, or we'll have to wait until tomorrow."

"Ooh, it's starting to sound like vampires again." Moki groaned and glanced around at some gravesites. "But seriously, bro, what *about* the window? And what tree? Details, bro, details."

Before Lanny could answer Moki, he saw Isabela walking rapidly toward the group, followed by a slim, middle-aged priest dressed in white vestments and carrying a large key ring. On it was a bunch of keys of various shapes and sizes. Tomás went to greet Father Pete. He soon introduced the man to the kids.

"Well, hello. Sorry for the delay," Father Pete said. "I

was officiating at an afternoon wedding that just ended. I've heard of you kids but never thought I'd get to meet you, let alone see you in action. This is the key you want." He handed it, ring and all, to Lanny, who thanked him.

The late-afternoon sun was still peeking around the corner of the cathedral and shining on the back of the mausoleum. *Perfect*, Lanny thought.

"Here, Ms. de Cordoba," Lanny said. He gave her the key. "I think you should be the one to unlock the door."

"Wait," Moki replied. "Just curious. So, it's all right to go around opening mausoleums?"

"Family members are allowed to do so, as are those conducting official business there with the family's knowledge, Moki," Father Pete replied with a smile and a nod.

Isabela unlocked the heavy iron door. Lanny pulled on it, and it opened with a screech. Cold, somewhat dank air reached his nostrils as he stepped inside, followed by the others. But it wasn't dark. Moki glanced at the dozen or more coffins on pedestals or tucked into shelves, bit his lower lip, and quickly looked at the floor.

"It's really bright in here," Rani whispered. Then, she snapped her fingers. "That's it. The 'improbable light' mentioned in the puzzle poem. Who would ever think it would be light in here? It was just as Lexi had figured."

"Check out the light source," Lanny said. "It's from the sunlight shining through the stained-glass window. I noticed the window this morning when we first searched here. Look familiar?"

Isabela's mouth dropped open. "Well, my goodness. It's the actual window from the movie *The Wedding*! My great-grandparents must have had it installed in here."

Tomás nodded. "We'll probably find a note about its installation in the family journal."

"So, that's what you saw that caused you to jump up and run over here?" Moki asked.

"That's it, bro. The afternoon sun is the 'radiant light' we had to await to make the window shine and show us the emerald." He gestured toward the window.

"The emerald! Where? Where?" Rani asked. She gazed intently at the stained glass.

"Where else? In the tree," Lanny replied.

He walked over and soon pointed to what appeared to be a large glass leaf near the top of the stained-glass image. There, radiating a bright green light, was a well-disguised though bulbous emerald, now obviously different from the other window-glass pieces.

Isabela exhaled deeply. "At last, and all this time, it's been right in front of us. How many times have we been in here, Tomás, and never even noticed the window had a Tree of Life design?"

"Too many times for too many family burials," Tomás replied. He caressed Lorenzo's and Alondra's caskets. "But it makes sense. The estate is named *La Casa de los Árboles*."

"Yes. Trees and, of course, lions fascinated our great-grandparents," she said.

"The emerald fits in well with that eternal Tree of Life design," Lanny said. "My fictional hero, Sherlock Holmes, always said the best place to hide something is right out in plain sight."

"I'd say you've learned well from your role model," Tomás replied.

Moki whistled. "So, that's what a multi-million-dollar, apricot-sized emerald looks like. And now we know why your great-grandfather had the security bars installed."

"Wo-o-o-w," Lexi and Rani said simultaneously. The sparkles in their eyes matched the gem.

"But wait a minute," Isabela said. She turned to the priest. "The mausoleum is no longer on our property, Father Pete. This emerald must belong to the cathedral or to the diocese now."

"Not quite. The grounds are the property of the diocese, but the gravesites and mausoleums belong to the families. The emerald is yours. Besides, you and your family have been more than generous to the cathedral and to the entire town over the years."

With the de Cordobas' permission, the kids took turns explaining to Father Pete about Isabela's plans and reasons for returning the gemstone to India.

The priest nodded his approval.

"Righting a wrong, even decades' old, is always gratifying," he said. "May blessings be upon you and your family. I will pray for you and for Olivia." The de Cordobas thanked him.

Moki gazed at the gemstone with his hands on his hips. "So, Ms. de Cordoba, now that we know the emerald is your property for the time being, how do we get it out of the window?"

Isabela smiled. "Just a little tree pruning should do it. But *mañana*—tomorrow." She looked askance at the boy, then winked. "We'll get a professional to do it, Moki, by daylight. It's been there for over seventy years. I doubt that it's going anywhere this evening."

"Ms. de Cordoba, is it all right to invite Aunt Connie over to photograph it?" Lexi asked. She knew this was an opportunity her aunt would not want to miss.

"Good thinking, Lexi. Of course. She'll want photos if she chooses to do a story about the Leticia Emerald."

The afternoon sun had just moved behind the cathedral, and the inside of the mausoleum was enshrouded in gathering twilight. Father Pete had everyone quickly circle and join hands. He said a brief blessing for the de Cordobas and their deceased ancestors. Then, all exited with Moki in the lead, and the iron door was locked. The priest congratulated the group and invited everyone to come to the cathedral soon for a tour and a celebration of life. Each agreed it was a fabulous idea.

The group walked back to the house. "Well, two cases solved on the same day," Isabela said to the kids. "You should be proud."

"Not yet," Lanny replied. "We have to get the emerald out and on its way home to India first."

"Hey, let's at least start planning the food for the St. Barnabas celebration," Moki said.

Lexi groaned. "Oh, Moki. You're too predictable to ever be mysterious."

CHAPTER TWENTY-FOUR

· ✧ ·

The Green-Eyed Monster

The de Cordobas and the kids were bursting to share the news that the emerald had been found. Instead, they chose to keep it a secret until the stone could be carefully excised from the window and shipped to its country of origin as Isabela intended. They also decided they would not answer any probable calls from the media in order to protect Olivia and her upcoming court case.

The morning after the emerald's discovery, the front page of the *Las Palmitas Gazette* was full of news about Olivia's and Madame Rouchard's arrests and the recovery of the gemstones of antiquity. Isabela, Tomás, the four detectives, Dr. Abbott, and Mr. Dayton were praised for their roles in solving the case. Sergeant Kalani was quoted often, having completed his initial interrogations.

Isabela gave the okay for the kids to read the story aloud as they sat in the living room and waited for Tina to finish preparing breakfast. All suspected the article would fill in much of the missing information for them about the two women and answer many questions that lingered at the time of their arrests. They weren't disappointed.

Lanny stared at his phone screen. "Listen to this about the thefts at the ARC:

In the hope of striking a deal with law enforcement for leniency, Olivia de Cordoba admitted falling in with international jewel thief Celeste Rouchard during college in France last year. Ms. de Corboba further said the woman took advantage of her vulnerability in the wake of her parents' deaths, and it was, therefore, easy to allow herself to be convinced the two should join forces to steal more gemstones. Being lonely and confused, she readily became fascinated with the thief's knowledge and technique and noticed that Celeste Rouchard was also a master of disguises. When the pair learned that the major "Gemstones of Antiquity" exhibition would arrive right in Las Palmitas, Olivia de Cordoba's hometown, the plan to steal the stones just seemed to drop into their laps."

Lanny continued:

"Police were able to discover how the two women gained access to the ARC and the display cases. Olivia de Cordoba had studied electronics in Europe and learned how to overcome security systems, unlock doors, and scramble security cameras. Next, the two came to the United States, attended the gemstone exhibition at its tour stop right before Las Palmitas, and stole the display case keys of an unsuspecting Mr. Christopher Dayton, the

exhibition curator. After quickly making duplicates, they slipped the originals back into his coat pocket.

Ms. de Cordoba further revealed that during their second ARC theft, it was Celeste Rouchard who knocked out the guard, Mr. Frank Abercrombie, to prevent his interference in their plans. She also admitted that her looks were slightly disguised by Madame Rouchard for the gemstone preview party many attended at the ARC, so neither Mr. Dayton nor anyone else would immediately recognize her. She was there to determine which stones the pair would steal next."

Lanny continued:

"The only thing Madame Rouchard would confess to was retrieving some old movie costumes, which Olivia de Cordoba had stolen from the de Cordoba mansion, from under a collapsed tombstone where the younger woman had hidden them in the St. Barnabas churchyard. Madame Rouchard's intent was to get the costumes to La Casa de los Árboles casita *quickly to sew on the stolen gemstones."*

Lanny concluded:

"This is a developing story. Check back later for more details."

Isabela snapped her fingers. "So, that must have been the day I saw Madame Rouchard walking hurriedly through the churchyard and carrying a bag."

Moki groaned and rubbed his neck.

At that moment, the doorbell rang. Tomás waved his sister off since she was still tired and went to answer it himself. The attorney, Troy Landis, could be heard in the entryway. Last night, the de Cordobas had called him to assist Olivia and to tell him about their finding the Leticia Emerald. Upon seeing him, Isabela rose, smiled broadly, and motioned him to a chair near her. He had just returned from talking with their cousin at the jail. Isabela gave him permission to share with the group what he had learned.

"There are some things Olivia wanted me to tell you," he began softly. He paused and clasped his hands. "She's very ashamed and is asking all of you to forgive her. She admits installing the old cassette recorder in the house's first floor passage. She heard all your plans about the emerald and recorded the puzzle poem reading."

Lanny and Lexi gave each other knowing looks.

Mr. Landis continued, "She's especially ashamed of dishonoring the family.

"Still harboring some anger over her parents' deaths, she tried to scare you by stomping around in Isabela's bedroom and on the third floor. She read Lorenzo's letter and the poem, too, but dropped them in Isabela's room when she heard you coming. She escaped through the secret passage there.

"She said she had foolishly shared what she knew about the Leticia Emerald with Madame Rouchard, who, of course, added that to their list of gems to steal. Olivia thinks her mind was poisoned against the family by Celeste Rouchard when the woman convinced Olivia that the emerald should have been inherited by *her* grandfather

Fernando since his father Marco had helped find it, and not by your great-grandfather Lorenzo, who hadn't gone to India with the others."

Lexi watched the de Cordobas stare at the floor, then said, "How sad. It's another example of the green-eyed monster devouring people's lives."

"'The green-eyed monster'?" Moki asked. "Are you referring to Madame Ronescu . . . er, Rouchard again?"

Lexi beat Lanny to the explanation. "No, Moki. Not Madame R." She rolled her eyes at him. "It's from Shakespeare's play, *Othello*. The green-eyed monster means 'jealousy.'"

Tomás suddenly asked, "Speaking of green, what about Olivia calling the emerald the 'Green Curse'? What made her change her mind and want to find it?"

"Celeste Rouchard," the attorney answered. "She also persuaded Olivia to focus on how rich they'd be, and how she could use the jewel to exact revenge finally on her family."

"I'd say the 'Green Curse' still touched her because nothing positive came of it," said Rani.

"By the way, Olivia complimented you kids on mostly keeping pace with her, if not forging ahead, on deciphering each puzzle poem stanza." Mr. Landis gave them a wry smile. The kids exchanged glances, not sure what to say. They weren't ones to accept praise easily.

Isabela smiled and nodded at them, easing their reluctance.

"And I'm so glad you kids did outsmart her," she said. "Maybe her lack of success with the emerald will ultimately help her case."

"Her team of attorneys will be using that very point during the trial," Troy said.

"Mr. Landis, did Ms. de Cordoba explain anything about how the daisies by the churchyard got trampled?" Lanny asked.

"Yes. She said she trampled them one rainy night when an owl startled her as she took a shortcut through the churchyard on her way to the *casita*. She lived there in the attic.

"And speaking of flowers, Isabela, she wanted me on her behalf to apologize to you especially for her taking the birthday bouquet of flowers you left on the mausoleum steps. At the time, she was angry that you were honoring the family—the family she was made to feel had wronged her over the emerald."

Isabela's eyes were downcast. "All the news is certainly sobering today. I'm glad we didn't share the finding of the Leticia Emerald—I mean, the *Temple Emerald*, with the world yet."

Tomás said, "Yes, the emerald. We need to give it its freedom in more ways than one."

CHAPTER TWENTY-FIVE

· ✧ ·

It's a Wrap

"**T**he sooner, the better," Isabela said.

She agreed with Tomás that they needed to excise the gemstone from the mausoleum window today. But she was glad Tina came in at that moment to announce breakfast. Mr. Landis's report about Olivia's confession had left the group in a slump, and it was in Isabela's nature to seek the positive. She led the group into the dining room.

As they sat down to waffles and home-grown blackberries, Rani said that she knew a great stained-glass artist. "Her name is Nikki Raymond. She designed, built, and installed a beautiful window at my house last year. I can call her for you."

"Perfect," Isabela said. "Let's keep our fingers crossed that she's available today."

Rani excused herself, located the artist's number, and called.

Upon returning to the table, she said, "Good news. Ms. Raymond will be here in one hour. And we can trust her to keep our secret."

"Even better still," Tomás said. He scraped the last drop of maple syrup from his plate.

"Oh, good," Moki said. "Time for one more waffle."

Lexi once again rolled her eyes at him.

Everyone was relieved that the town's news media were camped at the estate's front gate, nowhere near the churchyard. As long as they were only looking for news about the ARC thieves, they'd have no idea another stolen gemstone was hiding right next door. The plan to keep the emerald's discovery a secret for now seemed to be working. Isabela called Father Pete to ask him to unlock the mausoleum door right away, cautioning him not to draw any attention to himself. Aunt Connie and Nikki Raymond soon arrived.

As the group walked from the house to the cemetery, Lexi explained to Ms. Raymond that Aunt Connie was going to do a series of articles about the window, the emerald, the estate, and all the movie memorabilia they found so far. Then, Isabela shared some related family tales with Nikki, Connie, and Troy.

Once inside the mausoleum, Lexi had fun pointing out the emerald to the two amazed women.

"Scripts, props, stills, costumes, a window, the mansion,

and an emerald," Nikki Raymond said. "Wow. So then, let's get busy. Would someone please hand me that artist's knife?" Troy obliged her.

Everyone watched the tall young woman work on the window from her ladder perch while Aunt Connie snapped one shot after another. "I have to say I've never been asked to remove a gemstone from a window, let alone from inside a mausoleum, but not to worry. For the most part, I can use the same careful procedure that I would for excising a piece of glass. And what fascinating histories this stone and the window have had."

Twenty minutes later, Ms. Raymond announced, "Yes! That does it. Whoa! Safely freed from its seventy-year captivity. Here you go, Ms. de Cordoba."

She carefully handed the huge, legendary gemstone to Isabela, who could only stare at it as it weighed down the palm of her hand.

Then, Ms. Raymond expertly filled the hollow spot with a similarly colored piece of green stained-glass that no one would be able to distinguish from the surrounding pieces. Within the hour, she gathered her tools, pledged her secrecy, and left.

"Who wants to be the first to hold the emerald?" Isabela asked.

Lexi smiled at her best friend. "Rani should since it came from her country." Starting with Rani, each person took a turn holding the heavy dark green stone, turning it over to view it from every angle. All agreed that the

Temple Emerald was astonishingly beautiful—and huge.

Tomás said, "Not to bring anyone down, but I think it's important to remember that this emerald, like other famous gemstones, though beautiful, has a tragic history as well."

"You're right," Isabela replied. "First, it's stolen from the Indian temple. But thanks to the cultural minister's description in his letter, we can verify this is, indeed, that stone."

Troy nodded.

Isabela continued. "Then, decades later, Olivia attempts to steal it, along with the other stones. It's brought enough misery to my family. I'm absolutely determined to send it to Mr. Pandarva in New Delhi today. I'll call him first with the good news that it's been found and that he should watch for it in the mail. *Adiós*, Green Curse. Hooo-ray." Isabela kissed the stone in her clenched fist good-bye as Aunt Connie snapped some final shots.

A short time later, the de Cordobas and the four detectives successfully dodged the media by driving out a side gate. They entered a jewelry store on Jacaranda Street. Isabela hoped to get assistance in properly mailing the stone overseas. The kids enjoyed the surprised look on the face of Mr. Richards, the jeweler, when he gazed at the former Leticia Emerald. He gladly arranged for its shipment for the privilege of holding and appraising the enormous gem, which he said was worth over five million dollars. He offered to buy it, but Isabela turned him down. She glanced at the kids. "It's going back to where it belongs."

They chuckled and nodded in agreement. Lexi was careful to hug, not grip, Isabela's arm.

After the gemstone was prepared for shipment, everyone watched the special mail courier take the highly insured package in hand. At long last, the emerald was on its way home to India. They all high-fived, even getting Isabela to join in.

As the group left the jeweler's, Lanny said, "Okay, now we can officially say this case is closed." He raised his clenched fists over his head. Everyone joined him in a resounding cheer.

Ten minutes later, the group pulled up to the same side gate from which they'd left *La Casa de los Árboles*. They were inundated by the media, now frantic for information about the legendary Leticia Emerald. The de Cordobas and the kids looked at one another and said simultaneously, "Mr. Richards." Each agreed that the news of the emerald's discovery had to have been leaked by the jeweler, not by Nikki Raymond or Father Pete.

Fortunately, Troy had stayed at the house and appeared next to the driver's side of the car. Isabela sat there frozen with her eyes scanning the scene. He opened the door and whisked her, Tomás, and the kids through the gate and onto the property. "No comment right now," he repeated to the cluster of news seekers. "Please give the family some consideration. A statement will be issued soon."

Within a few minutes, the de Cordobas, the kids, and their rescuer were far from the din outside the gate. They each let out a deep sigh as they entered the quiet house through the back patio doors.

"Thanks, Troy. You're a life-saver," Isabela said. "I'm so done with that emerald."

While he and the de Cordobas went to the living room to discuss Olivia's situation further, the four kids started making calls to share the big news. Lexi called her mother and Dr. Abbott. Lanny called his father, Uncle Rocky, and Bruce. Rani and Moki called their parents.

An hour later, the house landline rang. It was Father Pete. "I think now would be a great time for all of you to come to St. Barnabas for the cathedral tour, celebration of life, and party," he said to Isabela. "I hope you're available. A large order of pizza has just arrived from a Dr. Abbott with a congratulatory note."

Soon, the happy group was inside the serene cathedral, a sharp contrast to the noisy media, which had finally dispersed. Each person marveled at the history of the beautiful High Gothic building as the monsignor led the tour. The squad had a new-found appreciation for the lofty stained-glass windows and the stories they revealed.

Then, Father Pete invited everyone into the rectory to enjoy the pizza treat. After they were seated, he offered a prayer of thanksgiving that the squad had solved both their cases and that Isabela had sent the emerald back to India. Finally, he served each guest a glass of frosty lemonade along with steaming hot pizza slices and pointed out the nearby platter of enormous chocolate chip cookies.

Moki chose to start his celebration with a cookie. Lexi stared at him. "You know what they say," he said. "Life is uncertain. Eat dessert first." Which he did, stuffing every crumb and chip into his mouth. It didn't take him long, however, to catch up with Lanny on the pizza.

After the feast, Isabela and Tomás presented each detective with an expensive-looking white card with gold edging. The note on it stated that soon, each of them would receive a special Eucalyptus Street mystery souvenir in the mail as a thank-you from the de Cordobas. When pressed, Isabela revealed that the gifts would be identical gold key rings with an emerald embedded in the center of a golden disk.

Moki spoke for the squad. "Cool. Thanks. And wow. An emerald, too."

Lanny said, "Thanks for your confidence in us since you obviously must have ordered the gifts before we even finished the case."

The others nodded and expressed their gratitude.

"And Lanny," said Isabela, "for being such a fan of our great-grandparents, we would like to present you with something extra." From behind her back, she produced a green felt, feathered hat.

"Wow, wow, and triple wow. Lorenzo's hat from *Robin Hood*! Thanks so much. This is going into a special storage box at home. I promise to take excellent care of it."

Isabela and Tomás smiled broadly.

Moki said, "My only regret about this case is that I didn't have time to make my famous pineapple-coconut upside-down cake for this party." He was still wiping melted cheese strings and pepperoni bits from his hands and face.

"My only regret is that our case is over," Lexi said. "I hope someone else hires us soon."

"I do, too, BFF," Rani said. "Plus, your aunt Connie is leaving tomorrow, so no more fancy-pants parties. No more dress up. Life could get pretty boring. And Moki and I might have to return to regular school."

Moki grinned. "Oh, I don't know. We don't do 'boring' very well. Something always comes up." He smiled and reached for another slice of pizza. "I happen to know for a fact that something evil is already unfolding just a few streets from here." He took a big bite, and through a mouthful of food, declared, "Might as well fill up while we can."

Laughing, Rani and Lanny joined him in more pizza.

"Whoa, Moki, whoa. Back up," Lexi said. She stood and planted her hands firmly on her hips. "You just said you 'know for a fact.' So, give. What's our next case? And where is it?"

With a cagey pause, the boy said, "Time will tell. . . . See, Lexi? I can be mysterious after all."

Kids—Thank you for buying and reading my book!

If you enjoyed it, I would love for you to _leave a review_ online. Reviews help other readers and inspire me.

I'd love to hear your _questions or comments, too_. You can contact me at **sherrilljoseph.com/contact**.

You can also sign up for my _monthly newsletter,_ geared mainly to kids, in order to follow the Botanic Hill Detectives at **sherrilljoseph.com/newsletter**.

And if you want to rejoin the Botanic Hill Detectives for the third adventure in the series, please watch for **Walnut Street: Phantom Rider** _coming soon in 2021_. Accompany your heroes as they head to a horse therapy ranch with a legendary, lost gold mine. A mysterious, frightening figure on horseback has been seen, and items are disappearing. And what's causing the strange lights and weird noises coming from the mountains? . . .

Until then, thanks. Read and write every day!

A BRIEF HISTORY OF
GEMSTONES OF ANTIQUITY

The popularity of gem material has changed considerably over the millennia. In ancient times, what were considered "precious" gemstones, like agate, jasper, and carnelian, would be considered "semi-precious" today. Such hierarchies, or orders of value, for gems weren't relevant and didn't even exist until the nineteenth century.

The ability to cut, facet, and polish stones to enhance their beauty is a relatively modern invention. In other words, sparkling diamond rings didn't exist in ancient times. Then, a diamond's value came from its hardness, durability, and purpose only. Emeralds were actually more desired.

Ancient gems had value based on their color and visual beauty, not on the types of materials that comprised them. For instance, red and blue stones, like carnelian and lapis lazuli, were especially popular and were often worn only by those of the highest social ranks. Some preferred solid bars of color in blue and orange tones.

The ancients also valued the opaqueness or semi-translucency of stones and their artistry, whereas cut and clarity are in demand today. Opaque stones were best for creating intaglios (concave images carved into stones), used for die stamping the "signatures" of nobility on important documents or wax seals; and, for cabochons (stones carved into domed, convex shapes) for jewelry.

Gemstones of antiquity were often used as religious symbols and talismans and valued for their purported medicinal values: Carnelians represented blood and protected the wearer from envy. Emeralds prevented blindness and eye diseases and had a soothing effect. Amethysts prevented inebriation. Lapis lazuli represented Heaven and divine favor. Peridots dissolved any spells or enchantments cast upon the wearer. Rubies were talismans of passion. Chrysoprase protected a thief from hanging. Amber released negative energy and cleared the mind.

There are many fascinating historical accounts of gemstones. Rome's Emperor Nero reportedly watched the gladiator fights while gazing through a giant emerald. Agates supposedly gave warriors strength and protection. Queen Cleopatra wore peridots while King Tut preferred turquoise and carnelian set in gold. The Bible mentions many "precious" stones such as jasper, sapphire,* chalcedony, emerald, sardonyx, sardius, beryl, and chrysolite (*Revelations* 21: 9–21).

Maybe you can find more such stories. Have fun researching!

Gemstones, no matter what their apparent value, have fascinated humankind for millennia.

---

*Biblical references to "sapphire" likely mean lapis lazuli.

The information for this and the following article was paraphrased from "The History and Mythology of Gemstones in Ancient Jewellery" at antiquities.co.uk, "Ancient History of the Gemstone" at faculty.washington.edu, and "Gemstone—Wikipedia" at en.m.wikipedia.org.

Purported Uses of Gemstones of Antiquity

adamas (diamond)—clear stone made of carbon; the hardest substance found in nature; the symbol of innocence and purity; thought by the Greeks to be the tears of the gods

agate—white to light gray with bands of color; protects and strengthens warriors

almandine garnet—scarlet and brown stone; unites passion and energy to heal

amber—golden fossilized tree resin; clears the mind and balances emotions

amethyst—purple stone of spirituality and peace; protects against poison and witchcraft; prevents inebriation

beryl—a single mineral with many color varieties, e.g., emerald, aquamarine, morganite

carnelian—orange to red glassy stone; gives courage and confidence to move forward

chalcedony—milky to colorful stone; enhances creativity, intellect, and energy

chrysolite (topaz)—golden-green to brown stone; signifies wisdom and charity

chrysoprase—golden-green stone; promotes happiness; heals depression and anxiety

coral—red to pink gemstone-quality variety of organic ocean coral; brings the wearer power

emerald—bright green stone; preserves love; brings prosperity and intuitive awareness; prevents blindness

faience—ceramic glass of melted feldspar stone; used for beads, small statues, and scarabs

fluorite—mineral form of calcium; many colors; promotes healing on all levels

heliotrope (bloodstone)—a green, red-spotted stone; used to stop bleeding; justice symbol

hematite—reddish-black stone; assists healing, fortune telling, meditation, and protection

jacinth—orange-red variety of zircon; eleventh of twelve stones in the Wall of Jerusalem

jasper—red, orange, brown, or green stone; brings stability, security, healing, and strength

lapis lazuli—bright blue stone mottled with white calcite and golden pyrite; one of the most sought-after stones in ancient times; symbol of royalty, power, honor, spirit, and vision

malachite—green stone with bands of dark to soft green; protects wearers from accidents

pearl—oldest known gem; organic matter from oysters and mollusks; symbol of purity, generosity, integrity, and loyalty; strengthens relationships and keeps children safe

peridot—green chrysolite; heals the healers; brings understanding of destiny and purpose

ruby—bright pink-red stone; protects home, wealth, and children; increases generosity; harbinger of passion

sard (sardius)—fiery blood-red stone; emblem of justice and vengeance

sardonyx—brown stone with white or brown-red veins; embodies optimism and stamina

serpentine—green, yellow-green, or brown-green spotted or veined stone; used in offerings to request blessings; protects against disease, evil sorcery, and the effects of snake venom

turquoise—opaque blue-green stone; symbol of friendship and truthful communication

ACKNOWLEDGMENTS

Dear Kids and Other Readers,

Part of the fun of writing is looking for ideas. This is called *inspiration.* Writers often get inspiration from art as well as from real life. An idea might be right in front of them—like an old fallen tree. A murky backyard pond. A spooky mask in a costume shop. Or a famous painting, musical piece, or movie.

Other stories can also inspire new ideas. In fact, three stories inspired me to write *Eucalyptus Street: Green Curse*. The first is a book by one of my favorite English novelists, Wilkie Collins, who lived from 1824 to 1889. In 1868, he wrote the novel, *The Moonstone*, generally considered to be the first detective novel. Its detective, Sergeant Cuff, searches an old country house for a fabulous yellow diamond, the Moonstone. We later learn that it was stolen from a temple in India.

Next, I must give a shout-out to Lanny's fictional detective hero Sherlock Holmes. The specific Holmes short story that inspired me is "The Musgrave Ritual," written by Sir Arthur Conan Doyle in 1893. You can find it in Doyle's story collection, *The Memoirs of Sherlock Holmes*. In the short story, Holmes uses a Musgrave family document, called the Musgrave Ritual, which is a set of questions and answers, to locate two people who have disappeared. He also finds . . . much more!

I could not leave out a mystery starring my favorite detective Nancy Drew. *The Hidden Staircase,* written in 1930, is my third literary inspiration. In that story, Nancy agrees to help solve a baffling mystery at an old stone mansion with a secret passage. The two women living there have heard strange noises and have seen shadows on the walls. Nancy knows the sources are real, not ghosts. So, why do they constantly elude her?

In conclusion, dear Readers, please keep your ears and eyes open for ideas to inspire your *own* writing. And when you read a story, see if you can find a connection to another story. That deepens your comprehension and appreciation of what you have read. So you see, writing and reading are inseparable. Keep practicing both.

Sherrill Joseph
San Diego, California

About the Author

Laurens Antoine Photography

Sherrill Joseph will be forever inspired by her beautiful students in the San Diego public schools where she taught for thirty-five years before retiring and becoming a published author.

She has peopled and themed the Botanic Hill Detectives Mysteries with children and adult characters of various abilities, races, cultures, and interests. Sherrill strongly believes that children need to find not only themselves in books but others from different races and social situations if all are to become tolerant, anti-racist world citizens. She also feels that kids are amazing human beings who don't tend to get enough credit from some adults for their blossoming insights and intelligence.

The author created her detectives—patterned after her own fifth-grade students and twelve-year-old twin cousins—to be mature, smart, polite role models that will appeal to parents, grandparents, teachers, and librarians, but especially to kids who seek the courage and self-respect needed to realize their greatest potential.

Sherrill is a lexical-gustatory synesthete and native San Diegan where she lives in a charming 1928 Spanish-style bungalow with her incredibly adorable poodle-bichon rescue, Jimmy Lambchop. Other loves include her daughter, son-in-law, granddaughter, dark chocolate, popcorn, old movies, purple, and daisies. Having never lived in a two-story house, she is naturally fascinated by staircases. Sherrill is a member of SCBWI and the Authors Guild and promises many more adventures with the squad to come.

CONNECT WITH SHERRILL
AND HER BOOKS AT—

SHERRILLJOSEPH.COM

AND ON—

TWITTER **@MYSTERYAUTHOR7**

INSTAGRAM **@SHERRILLJOSEPHAUTHOR**

FACEBOOK **@BHDMYSTERIESAUTHOR**

SUBSCRIBE TO HER
MONTHLY NEWSLETTER AT—

SHERRILLJOSEPH.COM/NEWSLETTER

Made in the USA
Las Vegas, NV
20 October 2020